This is not a

SCIENCE FICTION

textbook

Copyright © 2024 Goldsmiths Press
First published in 2024 by Goldsmiths Press
Goldsmiths, University of London, New Cross
London SE14 6NW

Copyright © 2024 Mark Bould and Steven Shaviro for selection and editorial material.
Chapter copyright belongs to individual contributors.

A CIP record for this book is available from the British Library.

ISBN 978-1-915983-09-1 (pbk)
ISBN 978-1-915983-10-7 (ebk)

Director, Goldsmiths Press: Sarah Kember
Publishing Consultant: Susan Kelly
Editorial and Production Manager: Angela Thompson
Publishing and Marketing Assistant: Kobe Reynders
Cover design: Crxss Design
Design: Heather Ryerson
Copyediting: Adriana Cloud
Printed and bound by Short Run Press Limited, UK

This book has been typeset in Neue Haas Grotesk Text Pro.

www.gold.ac.uk/goldsmiths-press

Goldsmiths
UNIVERSITY OF LONDON

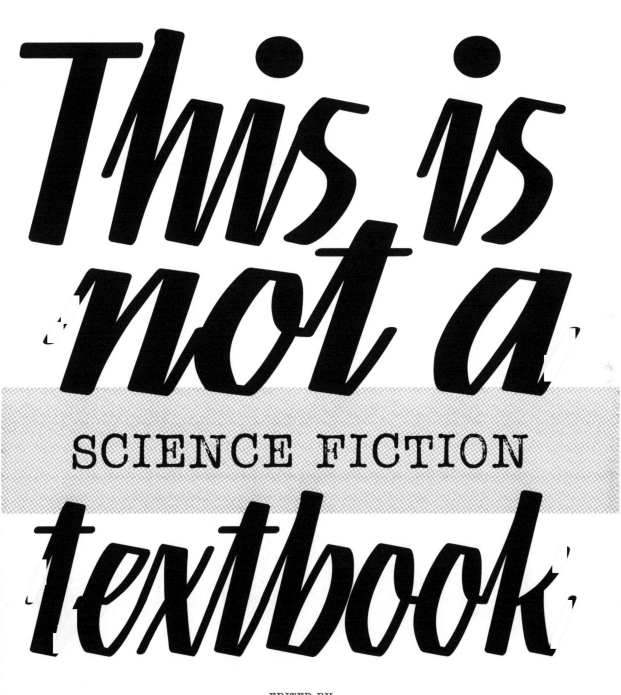

This is not a

SCIENCE FICTION

textbook

EDITED BY

MARK BOULD & STEVEN SHAVIRO

Goldsmiths
Press

Contents

Part Three: Key Concepts ↓

Introduction

STEVEN SHAVIRO

In all known societies, people have been enthralled by fantastic fiction: stories that depart from the familiarity of daily life and give rise to what is often called a 'sense of wonder'.

→ **But science fiction (sf) is primarily an invention of the modern, technocultural West.**

It first appeared in the work of such nineteenth-century writers as Mary Shelley, Edgar Allan Poe, Jules Verne and H.G. Wells, all of whom anticipated – in response to scientific discoveries – new ways of being. Sf became more widespread over the course of the twentieth century, along with a high pace of technological innovation and the growth of mass culture. Later in the twentieth century, sf passed from the margins to the mainstream and from prose fiction to other media, such as film, television and computer games. In the twenty-first century, sf is less a particular genre of entertainment than it is a mode: a manner of approach, a set of themes or a pervasive atmosphere, appearing in the most diverse contexts. Today, sf extends through all of culture and society. In a world of high-speed communications, ubiquitous computing, worldwide transmission of brands, memes and fads, and crazed multibillionaires spending vast sums of money on their own whims and fantasies, nearly all of human life takes on a science-fictional cast. We are living in the age of science-fictionalised reality.

This book is written out of our heightened awareness of these larger trends, but it focuses on the particular sort of invention that is found in sf literature and film. Sf in this narrower sense holds up a peculiar sort of mirror to our contemporary world: it reflects things back to us not as they actually are but as they might otherwise be. Sometimes sf extrapolates: it pushes existing conditions – like unending war, widespread surveillance or consumerist frenzy – to their logical extremes. Sometimes sf speculates: it uncovers incipient or hidden potentials – new sorts of sexual flourishing, novel technologies, strange climates – and imagines the differences their unfolding might make for the ways we live our lives. Still other times, sf fabulates: it imagines new sorts of stories, ones that do not merely replicate tired, overfamiliar narratives or fit into our customary patterns; as sf author Michael Swanwick puts it, 'The world is choking on old stories . . . . Tell new and better ones' (363).

Sf has its own repertoire of tropes, images and themes. It imagines alternative societies, both utopian and dystopian. It is filled with robots and androids who are able to outthink us, and with spaceships that use loopholes in the theory of relativity to travel faster than the speed of light. It narrates encounters with intelligent alien species from other planets. It explores the strategies that societies might use in order to mitigate, or at least adapt to, climate disruption and other existential threats. It envisions technologies which free us from resource scarcity, from the need to labour and even from mortality – but which do not necessarily resolve other basic human dilemmas. All these themes and images have permeated the larger culture and become familiar to everyone. But sf, by dwelling with them so intently, often explores their ramifications with impressive depth or twists them into previously unforeseen forms.

All these tropes are intrinsically double. On the one hand, they expand our imaginative reach, pointing towards otherwise unanticipated developments. Sf writers themselves have often said that they do not claim to predict the future; rather, they open up possibilities and alternatives that are contingent, risky and uncertain – things and events that could never be predicted with any certainty. On the other hand, yet also at the same time, sf's tropes resonate strongly with actual conditions. Alien encounter stories, for instance, recall traumatic colonial encounters between Europeans and Indigenous peoples from other parts of the world. As Toni Morrison once pointed out, what could be more science-fictional than the experiences of Africans who found themselves kidnapped by odd-looking strangers with powerful technologies, who transported them elsewhere and either murdered them or put them to work as slaves? The modern capitalist world was founded by such unimaginable ventures whose effects still shape society. In this way, sf is grounded in the past and present, even as it flies off into potential futures. Sf novelist Kim Stanley Robinson compares sf to the 'special glasses' we wear in order to watch 3D movies: 'one lens of science fiction is a real attempt to imagine a possible future. The other lens is a metaphor for the way things are right now' (Plotz), and sf is what happens when these two different images coalesce into a view of greater depth.

Sf writers open up possibilities and alternatives that are contingent, risky and uncertain

Writing books is something that authors can do entirely alone – even getting books published is a relatively low-cost endeavour – but it is still difficult for them to make a living solely from their writing. Film production and game development, in contrast, require large numbers of people to work together, but their imaginative activity is always subject to massive economic constraints. So whatever else sf might do, it cannot avoid also being crassly commercial. Perhaps this makes sf all the more relevant, both to our actual situation in the world and to our desires to negate the world's limitations and disappointments. Actuality and escapism go together in sf in a way that would be impossible in more conventionally realistic modes of expression or representation. Consequently, this volume offers an introduction not only to sf's stunning imaginative reach, but also to its compromises and disappointments.

How to use this book

MARK BOULD

Any way you want to. Seriously.

We've designed it so every chapter stands on its own (although the final section does contain paired chapters).

So dip in where you please or work through it systematically. Start with something you're interested in or with something you have never even heard of. Go off on tangents. Disappear down rabbit holes. Whatever works for you.

The book has three sections. 'Theory' outlines some key ideas that help us think about sf. 'History' outlines some of the contexts from which sf emerged and how it evolved. 'Key Concepts in Contemporary Sf' contains twenty-two pairs of chapters, each of which introduces a way of thinking about the genre and a relevant recent sf text. Although 'History' ends around 1980, its final chapter slingshots into the new millennium, and 'Key Concepts' covers much of the genre's subsequent development.

All 'further reading' and 'further viewing' recommendations – along with everything else in text boxes – are the work of the editors, not our authors. We did this to minimise repetition across the book, and to ensure writers, directors, books and films were not ghettoised. For example, it would badly misrepresent the genre to only list African American authors under 'Afrofuturism' or space operas only under 'space opera'.

Although we focus on novels and feature films, we do also refer to and/or recommend novellas, short stories, collections, anthologies, comics, YA fiction, short films, animation, speculative documentaries and TV shows. Some of the titles we mention are exemplary works, while others are just good and useful examples. But we're not going to tell you which is which. Make up your own mind (we probably don't agree with each other anyway).

Also, we have adopted a broad and generous approach to the genre, so you might consider some of the titles to not even be sf – even if other people do. And thinking about how different people understand texts differently is far more rewarding than a turf war.

Any title followed by an asterisk is part of a series, usually but not always its first instalment. To save space, we've dropped most subtitles, but we've retained a handful for clarity. And almost every title we refer to is currently in print, in physical and/or digital formats, and many will be available free from your local library: use it or lose it.

Part

THEORY

→ Genre

MARK BOULD

What is genre? And why does no one agree?

Genre seems like a simple idea, but it is full of contradictions and bound up in the cultural politics of taste.

The term is used to describe forms (e.g. poetry, drama, prose), but also varieties of those forms (e.g. epic or lyric, tragedy or comedy, fiction or nonfiction, realism or romance) and commercial categories (e.g. sf, crime, westerns). Producers and consumers often have conflicting notions of what properly belongs within these categories, which can look very different in different media.

'Genre' is also often used in an elitist manner, to distinguish the debased formulaic fiction, full of shock and sentiment, supposedly preferred by unsubtle working-class and female readers, from the nuanced 'literary fiction' purportedly favoured by the more refined palate of the educated middle class.

Furthermore, while treating genres as pigeonholes might be useful for shelving purposes, in reality any novel, film or TV show contains elements drawn from and associated with multiple different genres. Often, one set of generic elements will appear dominant, but not always. For example, compare Philip K. Dick's *The Man in the High Castle* (1962) with Haruki Murakami's *IQ84* (2009–10). Dick imagines a world in which Germany and Japan won World War II, and maps out some of the geopolitical, social and psychological consequences; Murakami invokes the sf conventions of alternate histories and parallel worlds to generate the sense of the uncanny that gives licence to the novel's hauntings, reincarnations, superhuman powers and fantastical beings, none of which are rationally motivated or explained. While few would dispute that Dick's novel is sf, that is partly because he wrote primarily – and prolifically – for sf magazines and paperback lines, winning three Hugo awards and being nominated for five Nebulas. However, it is easy to imagine an alternate timeline in which his novel was not pre-emptively framed in this way but appeared without generic labelling as a mainstream literary novel. In contrast, if you claim *IQ84* as sf, you can expect resistance from two directions. First, Murakami is published as a literary author and frequently rumoured to be a Nobel Prize nominee, so his work is routinely labelled not as sf but as 'postmodernist' or 'magical realist' because he tends to blend multiple genres together and to introduce fantastical elements into realist settings. Second, if *IQ84* is sf, it is not very good sf: it fails to build significantly upon the protagonist's sudden realisation that police uniforms and firearms are unfamiliar, let alone imagine any consequence at all of its alternative Earth having two moons.

However, even if one set of generic elements seems dominant, as in Dick's novel, there is no objective position from which to make this judgement. We all occupy specific social positions and have particular life histories that shape the way we make sense of a text. For example, in IMDb user comments on David Cronenberg's sf-horror hybrid *The Fly* (1989), you will find sf fans attributing all its positive qualities to sf and its negative ones to horror, and horror fans doing precisely the opposite, while others, unfamiliar with the affordances and accomplishments of sf and horror, express surprise at its effectiveness and feel obliged therefore to claim that it somehow 'transcends' genre.

So is it sf?

- *Upstream Color* (Carruth 2013)
- *Hard to Be a God* (German 2013)
- *Seconds* (Frankenheimer 1966)
- *The Face of Another* (Teshigahara 1966)
- *Last Year at Marienbad* (Resnais 1961)

MARK BOULD

What is sf? And why does no one agree?

While most people seem pretty certain what they mean when they discuss a genre, it is impossible to compose a definition that works.

There are problems of circularity, situatedness, focus and consensus. To define a genre, you must already know what it contains, but to know what it contains you must already have defined it. Definitions are construed from specific positions, none of which possess perfect knowledge of the genre and all of which have different priorities and purposes. Definitions negotiate between broad applicability and narrow specificity, and thus between inclusive and exclusive versions of the genre; but if a definition is too expansive, it becomes meaninglessly vague, and if it is too particular, it excludes texts many would include. And any definition is just one among many, so even if you are persuaded by it, there is no reason to believe others will be.

Nonetheless, definitions are useful. They articulate a perspective on and organise our understanding of a genre. For example, Hugo Gernsback's editorial in the first issue of *Amazing Stories* (1926–2005) defined sf as 'the Jules Verne, H.G. Wells and Edgar Allan Poe type of story – a charming romance intermingled with scientific fact and prophetic vision' (3). Since this was the debut issue of the first pulp magazine devoted entirely to sf, Gernsback had to assert that this new commercial category – which he called 'scientifiction' – already existed in some way. So he concocted a selective tradition by yoking together two best-selling, world-famous European authors who vehemently denied writing the same kind of fiction as each other, and an American who was more celebrated in Europe and better known for his horror fiction. Gernsback also mentions American

> **The Jules Verne, H.G. Wells and Edgar Allan Poe type of story – a charming romance intermingled with scientific fact and prophetic vision**

Edward Bellamy, whose *Looking Backward* (1888) prompted the massive late nineteenth-century outpouring of utopian fiction, but does not refer to any of the popular American authors, such as Edgar Rice Burroughs, Jack London, George Allan England and Francis Stevens, who had already written sf for general fiction magazines. This editorial – a pitch to readers, a prospectus for contributors – thus positions sf in relation to famous authors and competitor magazines. It implies that sf has a lineage but is forward-looking; that sf is American, but international, not parochial; and that sf is popular but respectable, appealing to pulp sensation but also rising above it, with scientific rationality grounding its flights of fancy in reality.

However, Gernsback's apparently simple formula does not indicate the relative proportions of charming romance, scientific fact and prophetic vision sf should contain. And even if you could reduce Verne, Wells, Poe and Bellamy to these elements, they each deploy them in multiple different combinations, providing varied and contradictory models. So while Gernsback's definition seems to nail things down, it also throws them wide open – it is a set of restrictions *and* a field of possibilities.

Any definition organises the genre around specific key texts and authors, and marginalises or excludes others. For example, champions of the sf associated with Robert A. Heinlein, Isaac Asimov and John W. Campbell's *Astounding* magazine (1930–) in the 1940s and 1950s implicitly and explicitly denigrated other popular forms of sf, such as planetary romances and space operas. The former, exemplified by C.L. Moore and Leigh Brackett and often found in *Weird Tales* (1923–54) and *Planet Stories* (1939–55), typically features human adventurers on alien planets encountering exotic remnants of ancient civilisations whose technology looks a lot like magic. The latter,

---

Science fiction is ...

'literature which deals with the reaction of human beings to changes in science and technology' – Isaac Asimov

'Something that could happen – but you usually wouldn't want it to' – Arthur C. Clarke

'the improbable made possible' – Rod Serling

'what we point to when we say it' – Damon Knight

'the literature of cognitive estrangement' – Darko Suvin

exemplified by E.E. 'Doc' Smith, Edmond Hamilton and Jack Williamson and found in *Weird Tales, Amazing* and *Astounding* (even under Campbell), features space battles between humans and aliens across and beyond the solar system. By casting such fiction as 'bad others', Campbellian sf laid claim to seriousness of purpose and maturity of taste.

However, genres change over time. The planetary romance developed less fanciful forms, such as Hal Clement's hard sf *Mission of Gravity* (1953),* published by Campbell, and Ursula K. Le Guin's anthropological *The Left Hand of Darkness* (1969).* Asimov's Foundation trilogy* (1942–51) is Campbellian space opera, and space opera was later embraced by Afrofuturist, feminist and literary writers, as in Samuel R. Delany's *Nova* (1968), Cecelia Holland's *Floating Worlds* (1976) and Colin Greenland's *Take Back Plenty* (1990),* as well as by hard sf, as in David Brin's *Startide Rising* (1983)* and Catherine Asaro's *Spherical Harmonic* (2001).*

Literary fiction often positions sf as its 'bad other', claiming a particular novel is not sf but 'speculative fiction', a distinction often reinforced by claiming that it is based in real possibilities, unlike the caricature of sf to which it is opposed. Ironically, 'speculative fiction' actually comes from the heartlands of American sf: Heinlein, one of the first sf writers to break out of the pulp magazines, used it to redefine himself against the juvenile sensationalism attributed to the pulps. Judith Merril, an sf writer turned editor, adopted the term to promote the more literary and experimental sf of 1960s and 1970s New Wave sf. Thus 'speculative fiction' has always played a role in patrolling, expanding or resisting the reach of sf. Two more recent terms that perform similar functions are 'slipstream' and 'lab lit'.

Slipstream, coined by cyberpunk Bruce Sterling in 1989, describes postmodern, metafictional or magic realist works that are not exactly sf but in some way feel like sf: 'a kind of writing which simply makes you feel very strange; the way that living in the twentieth century makes you feel, if you are a person of a certain sensibility' (78). It drew major literary authors, such as Isabel Allende, William Burroughs, Gabriel García Márquez, Toni Morrison and Thomas Pynchon, into the borderlands of the genre. Examples include Ishmael Reed's *Mumbo Jumbo* (1972), Alasdair Gray's *Lanark* (1981), Angela Carter's *Nights at the Circus* (1984), Don DeLillo's *White Noise* (1985), William T. Vollmann's *You Bright and Risen Angels* (1987), Katherine Dunn's *Geek Love* (1989) and Gerald Vizenor's *The Heirs of Columbus* (1991).

Lab lit depicts scientists and laboratory culture in realistic historical or contemporary settings but generally eschews scientific speculation. Its prestigious lineage includes Honoré de Balzac's *The Quest of the Absolute* (1834), Thomas Hardy's *Two on a Tower* (1882), Émile Zola's *Doctor Pascal* (1893), Sinclair Lewis' *Arrowsmith* (1925), Pearl S. Buck's *Command the Morning* (1959) and DeLillo's *Ratner's Star* (1977), but the term was coined – by Jennifer Rohn – only in 2001. Her LabLit.com site struggles to segregate it from sf. Novels such as Gwyneth Jones' *Life* (2004), Andy Weir's *The Martian* (2011) and Kim Stanley Robinson's *Science in the Capital* trilogy (2004–7) appear on her main list, rather than among her 'crossover' list of sf, technothrillers, adventure fiction and magic realism. This is not so much an error as a consequence of reading

'Speculative fiction' has always played a role in patrolling, expanding or resisting the reach of sf

them from a lab lit perspective. They are novels with, respectively, a relatively small speculative element (albeit with massive implications), an engineering approach to scientific problem-solving, and a focus on the way policy, politics and institutions determine scientific practice. But just because, seen this way, they are lab lit does not mean that they are not also sf (and vice versa).

MARK BOULD

The world as it is but made strange. And seen more clearly.

In 1917, Russian critic Viktor Shklovksy coined the term *ostranenie* (defamiliarisation) to describe poetic language's ability to disrupt habitual perceptions of the world. By making things seem strange and new, poetry's unexpected word choices, unusual rhythms and piquant images break through the unquestioned assumptions of everyday life and create a fresh relationship with the real.

Around the same time, German philosopher Ernst Bloch began to use *Novum* (new thing) to describe a moment in human history that startles us out of accepting the world as it is and awakens us to the possibility of change.

In 1935, German playwright Bertolt Brecht coined *Verfremdungseffekt* (alienation effect) to describe the aim of his revolutionary performance and staging strategies. By undermining the illusory reality of the play's fictional world and blocking identification with characters' emotions, he hoped to engage audiences intellectually, prompting them to turn these newly awoken critical capacities onto the world outside the theatre.

In the 1970s, Darko Suvin adapted and merged these concepts to argue that sf defamiliarises, alienates or estranges the world, and does so by organising the text around a novum – typically a scientific or technological innovation – that transforms the world of conventional realist fiction into one that is sufficiently familiar to be understood but also radically different. Suvin argued that, unlike the worlds of fantasy or supernatural horror or magic realism, an sf world is 'cognitively estranged' – that is, scientifically plausible and coherently developed. For example, Franz Kafka's 'The Metamorphosis' (1915) is not sf because, when Gregor Samsa wakes up mysteriously transformed into a bug, there is no rational explanation of how or why this impossible change has occurred. But H.G. Wells' *The Island of Doctor Moreau* (1896) is sf because the Beast Folk are products of the scalpel-wielding scientist's surgical interventions. A game of Quidditch is not sf because Harry Potter and his chums fly around on broomsticks at a school of witchcraft and wizardry, but a Rollerball match is sf because, although there is nothing futuristic about the players' motorbikes and roller skates, it takes place in a dystopian future dominated by global corporations – and obeys the laws of physics.

Carl Freedman and China Miéville offer important correctives to Suvin's argument. Sf is not necessarily concerned with actual scientific cognition but depends upon rhetorical strategies to produce a 'cognition effect'; it is not so much about science as charismatic persuasion. That is, while vivisection could never transform animals into human-like beings, Wells uses the language and imagery of science to generate a particular kind of plausibility.

Different writers employ different modes of persuasion, though, and readers often use this to make value judgements about specific texts. For example, Wells' *The Time Machine* (1895) relies upon a rhetorically heightened tautology: time is the fourth dimension, so time travel is made possible by 'dimensional quadrature', that is, by traveling in the fourth dimension. Gregory Benford's hard-sf *Timescape* (1980) entirely rules out the possibility of time travel, instead exploring how tachyons, hypothetical subatomic particles that travel faster than light and thus backwards in time, might be used to communicate an urgent warning to the past. Toshikazu Kawaguchi's *Before the Coffee Gets Cold* (2015)* is structured around a set of rules limiting time travel but offers no explanation of how it is possible – and thus is arguably not sf at all.

Estranged worlds

- Rivers Solomon, *Sorrowland* (2021)
- Agustina Bazterrica, *Tender Is the Flesh* (2017)
- China Miéville, *The City & the City* (2009)
- Colson Whitehead, *The Intuitionist* (1999)
- J.G. Ballard, *High-Rise* (1975)

Estranged worlds on screen

- *In Time* (Niccol 2011)
- *A Scanner Darkly* (Linklater 2006)
- *Possible Worlds* (Lepage 2000)
- *Punishment Park* (Watkins 1971)
- *Invasion of the Body Snatchers* (Siegel 1956)

MARK BOULD

What will happen if this – or that – goes on?

In mathematics, extrapolation describes a method of estimating the value of a variable in relation to known data points. As the pulps matured, sf adopted the term to explain a method of developing story ideas – that is, asking what implications and consequences can reasonably be expected from a particular trend continuing or from a novel event (e.g. a scientific discovery or new technology) occurring.

For example, Isaac Asimov's 'The Endochronic Properties of Resublimated Thiotimoline' (1948) and its three sequels (1952, 1959, 1973) were inspired by his observation in a lab of the speed with which catechol dissolves in water – so fast that if it were any quicker, it would dissolve before the water touched it. In effect, he maps a series of known data points (the solubility rates of different chemical compounds) on a graph and extends the line that runs through them to extrapolate the existence of a compound that somehow anticipates the addition of water and dissolves before contact. He then extrapolates from the observed behaviour of the imaginary Thiotimoline to work out what kind of chemical structure it must possess to act in this way: each of its molecules is so densely packed that its carbon atom takes on a unique form, in which four of its six chemical bonds exist in normal space-time, but one bond extends into the past and one into the future, enabling it to anticipate the addition of water. The first extrapolation moves *from* the real-world *to* a science-fictional one in which Thiotimoline exists; the second, *from* the characteristics of the fictional world required for the story *to* the rationale that makes them plausible.

However, Asimov still does not have a story, so he must extrapolate the narrative potentials of his novum – the difficulty

> **What implications and consequences can reasonably be expected from a particular trend continuing or from a novel event occurring?**

of doing so is attested to by the fact that the four Thiotimoline stories take the form of spoof scientific papers and speeches. In them, experimenters learn that when they attempt to trick Thiotimoline by preventing the intended addition of water from actually happening, some accident occurs to ensure it does, including hurricanes and floods, which converts the innocent compound into a weapon of mass meteorological destruction. Also, because of those unique carbon bonds, Thiotimoline tricked into dissolving might move forward or backward in time in search of water, enabling time travel.

Some sf shies away from extrapolated consequences, as when the potentially world-changing textiles innovation in *The Man in the White Suit* (Mackendrick 1951) is destroyed before its far-reaching impact can be felt. Some sf, such as Paolo Bacigalupi's *The Water Knife* (2015) and Kim Stanley Robinson's *The Ministry for the Future* (2020), takes them very seriously indeed. Some does not so much extrapolate from as exaggerate aspects of contemporary life to satirical ends, such as Frederik Pohl and Cyril Kornbluth's *The Space Merchants* (1953). And some use these strategies of accentuation to issue dire warnings: Orwell's *Nineteen Eighty-Four* (1949) satirises Stalinism to draw out the authoritarian tendencies of post-war austerity Britain – extrapolating from the former to estrange the latter.

Fredric Jameson turns much of this on its head, ignoring sf's claims about compositional methodology to instead focus on the experience of reading an sf text. Because the text must be comprehensible to the reader, the novum and its extrapolated consequences must stand against a more or less conventionally realistic depiction of the world. He argues therefore that 'extrapolation' better describes the recombination and juxtaposition of varied and contradictory elements of the real world into striking montages.

Satirical extrapolations

- Joanna Kavenna, *Zed* (2019)
- Tricia Sullivan, *Maul* (2004)
- Carol Emshwiller, *Carmen Dog* (1988)
- J.G. Ballard, *Crash* (1973)
- Bernard Wolfe, *Limbo* (1952)

Onscreen satirical extrapolations

- *Antiviral* (Cronenberg 2012)
- *Black Mirror* (2011–)
- *RoboCop* (Verhoeven 1987)*
- *The Model Couple* (Klein 1977)
- *Dr Strangelove* (Kubrick 1964)

→ | Alterity

MARK BOULD

Aliens, robots, future worlds – imagining difference reveals the self.

'Alterity' describes the sense of the Other as distinct from the Self. The Other cannot really be known since the Self cannot experience it directly, but the Self needs the Other in order to determine where its own borders lie. This uncertain dialectical process of negotiating boundaries and identities does not operate just on the level of individuals.

In Stanislaw Lem's *Solaris* (1961), over a century has passed since humans discovered the eponymous planet, which is occupied solely by an ocean of sentient metamorphic plasma. In all that time, there has been no successful communication. The science of Solaristics, with decades of experimental results, hypotheses, approaches, controversies and paradigm shifts, can say nothing definitive about the vast gelatinous alien but does reveal an awful lot about human concerns and priorities. The alien also does not understand the humans studying it, so its attempts to communicate only cause them anguish. Ultimately, when the protagonist reaches out his hand to the ocean, it forms a limb to return the gesture, but they remain just two Selves mutually defining themselves against an Other they do not comprehend.

Real-world colonial encounters were rarely so phlegmatic. Typically, European colonisers construed Indigenous peoples not just as Other, but as an inferior Other: savage, irrational, barely human – unlike the colonising Self, which considered itself civilised, rational and fully human. The Other culture was thus deemed a lesser object to be studied, and in obvious need of the modernising governance that only the coloniser could provide. Such attitudes became institutionalised, reiterated constantly by governments, media, education and religion until they became commonplace, circulating without comment through the fabric of daily life. Of course, at the same time, they were and are contested, not least by those so Othered.

Sf has been deeply involved in such Othering processes, but also in challenging them. Whether depicting race, ethnicity, class, gender, sexuality, ability or species, it often unthinkingly, and sometimes deliberately, reiterates the perspective of the dominant term in each hierarchical opposition. But sf has also produced and repeatedly deploys an array of devices, such as robots and aliens, for sympathetically exploring Otherness.

At the same time, since the Other is largely a fiction created by the Self, the construction of alterity tends to be much more about the Self than its imagined opposite. For example, *Invasion of the Body Snatchers* (Siegel 1956) is often described as a McCarthy-era allegory about the Communist menace invisibly infiltrating America. However, beyond its paranoid mood, there is little if anything in the film to support this reading. Rather than revealing Reds under the bed, it repeatedly draws attention to post-war commodity culture destroying 'authentic' experiences (a jukebox replaces a live band) and to conservative suburban morality stifling 'real' feeling. The very fact that the alien Pods can be mistaken for communists suggests the extent to which some viewers are unable to admit to the dull conformism of their own culture, with its fantasies of freedom and individualism.

Encountering otherness

- Aliya Whiteley, *Skyward Inn* (2021)
- Adam Roberts, *The Thing Itself* (2015)
- Nnedi Okorafor, *Lagoon* (2014)
- Molly Gloss, *Wild Life* (2000)
- Arkady and Boris Strugatsky, *Roadside Picnic* (1972)

Encountering otherness on screen

- *Under the Skin* (Glazer 2013)
- *Wild Blue Yonder* (Herzog 2007)
- *Doppelganger* (Kurosawa 2003)
- *The Fly* (Cronenberg 1986)
- *The Thing* (Carpenter 1982)

→ | Historicising the present

MARK BOULD

Possible futures are all about the world as it now exists.

György Lukács' *The Historical Novel* (1937) argues that human consciousness of history as a constant ongoing process of change was relatively underdeveloped until the massive upheavals of the French Revolution (1789–99) and the Napoleonic Wars (1803–15). In response, a new genre of historical fiction emerged that, with Sir Walter Scott, Honoré de Balzac and Leo Tolstoy, recognised the scale and processes of social transformation. They abandoned any sense of earlier periods as static backdrops, instead depicting history as the unfolding of potentialities and populating their fiction with characters who embodied the contradictions of their times. Scott, for example, constantly returns to tension between Scotland's Highland clans and Lowland commerce, mapping the collapse of feudalism and the aristocracy against the rise of capitalism and the bourgeoisie.

For Lukács, the violent suppression of the 1848 European revolutions signalled the demise of the bourgeoisie as a revolutionary class, and consequently the end of the historical novel's vision of society as unstable, contingent, complexly determined and full of transformative potential. Carl Freedman's *Critical Theory and Science Fiction* (2000) argues that sf took over this critical historicising project. For example, Mary Shelley's *Frankenstein* (1818) is set in the recent past; the creature, twice compared to a mummy, recalls a lingering ancient past; and in Victor's feverish imagination, the creature's potential offspring foreshadow a future of proletarian and anti-colonial revolution. H.G. Wells' *The Time Machine* (1895) projects its protagonist into the year 802701. But the Time Traveller's speculations about the nature of this future society, and the revelations about how it actually works, are rooted in late-Victorian potentialities. While the landscape indicates

The future is a place of alterity, where continuity and change are brought into play so as to draw out the contradictions of the present

the triumph of agrarian socialism over capitalism, its population suggests that economic classes have split into distinct species: simple childlike Eloi, descended from an effete aristocracy and leisured bourgeoisie; and simian subterranean Morlocks, descended from workers, who maintain the infrastructure and raise the Eloi for meat. Wells does not intend this as a prediction. In sf, the future is a place of alterity, where continuity and change are brought into play so as to draw out the contradictions of the present – most obviously in satirical or cautionary tales, such as Ray Bradbury's *Fahrenheit 451* (1953) or Harry Harrison's *Make Room! Make Room!* (1966).

Historical novels and sf both estrange the present: the former show how it was determined by complex ongoing material processes operating in the past, the latter imagines possible futures that foreground such processes operating now. Indeed, the plausibility of many sf texts depends upon how persuasively the futures they depict are derived from contemporary trends. Futurologically motivated sf, such as John Brunner's *The Shockwave Rider* (1975) and David Brin's *Earth* (1990), tend to anticipate some real-world developments but fall victim to the rapid divergence of actual history. In contrast, although the precise social organisation outlined in Margaret Atwood's *The Handmaid's Tale* (1985) remains improbable, the current context of white supremacism, right-wing fundamentalism and attacks on female bodily autonomy and reproductive health render its broader vision of the future US increasingly credible.

Future histories

- Doris Lessing, *Shikasta* (1979)*
- Cordwainer Smith, *Instrumentality of Mankind* stories (1950–93)
- H.G. Wells, *The Shape of Things to Come* (1933)
- Olaf Stapledon, *Last and First Men* (1930)*
- Alfred Döblin, *Mountains Oceans Giants* (1924)

MARK BOULD

The door dilated. Her world exploded. He turned on his side.

By imagining different futures and other worlds, sf sets itself a unique linguistic task; no other genre must so concern itself with the naming of things that do not yet and might never actually exist. The creation of these new words has two sometimes overlapping forms.

Neosemes are familiar words that have come to mean something quite different in their new sf context. For example, in Charles Stross' *Accelerando* (2005) 'identity theft' refers to stealing the drive on which someone's uploaded consciousness is running. Less flippantly, in Philip K. Dick's *Ubik* (1969), 'half-life' refers not to the rate at which radioactive elements decay but to a period of 'cold pac' suspended animation during which the recently deceased can be fleetingly restored to consciousness to consult with the bereaved.

Neologisms are newly created words, usually extrapolated from existing languages. Karel Čapek's *R.U.R.* (1920) introduced 'robot', derived from the Czech for 'forced labour'; Jack Williamson's 'Collision Orbit' (1952) coined the verb 'to terraform'; malicious software was first described as a 'virus' in David Gerrold's *When H.A.R.L.I.E. Was One* (1972); and William Gibson's 'Burning Chrome' (1982) gave us 'cyberspace'.

The distinction between neologisms and neosemes is not always clear-cut. For example, Philip K. Dick often calls airborne cars 'flivvers', which is presumably short for 'flying vehicles'. However, 'flivver' was also a common nickname for the Model T Ford, so by redeploying the word more than a quarter of a century after production of the car ceased, Dick also connotes the mass-produced, the old-fashioned, the rickety and the poorly maintained. ('Flivver' was also the name of the single-seater 'everyman's airplane' Ford developed to prototype stage in the late 1920s.)

Neosemes and neologisms are examples of the way sf worlds negotiate between continuity and change, identity and alterity. Sometimes sf pushes this to more elaborate and challenging extremes. Nadsat, the fictional slang spoken by English youth gangs and in which Anthony Burgess' *A Clockwork Orange* (1962) is written, is crammed with Russian loanwords, adopted and adapted as part of the droogs' incoherent, if nonetheless eloquent, resistance to authority. Russell Hoban's *Riddley Walker* (1980) is told in the supposedly degraded but playful and poetic English of those eking out an existence three hundred years after the nuclear holocaust, while Jack Womack's cyberpunk *Random Acts of Senseless Violence* (1993)* charts future evolutions of American English. *The Expanse* (2015–22) divides the future solar system between three rival powers: Earth, Mars and the Outer Planets. The last group, who have colonised the asteroid belt and the moons of Jupiter and Saturn, are known as 'Belters' and they speak a distinctive diasporic polyglot creole of Arabic, Chinese, English, French, German, Hebrew, Italian, Japanese, Persian, Polish, Portuguese, Russian, Spanish, Swedish, Ukrainian, Zulu and other languages, which the series neither translates nor subtitles. When viewers first encounter this lang Belta, they might only recognise fragments, but through context and repetition, they begin to learn their way not only into an alternative language but also a different worldview to that of the more or less standard English spoken by welwala Inners.

Sf about language

- Harry Josephine Giles, *Deep Wheel Orcadia* (2021)
- China Miéville, *Embassytown* (2011)
- Suzette Haden Elgin, *Native Tongue* (1984)*
- Ian Watson, *The Embedding* (1973)
- Samuel R. Delany, *Babel-17* (1966)

MARK BOULD

Scale. Speed. Colour. Motion. Detail. Multiplied. And turned up to eleven.

Sf inherited the Gothic's preoccupation with the sublime – the encounter with a phenomenon of such magnitude that it stuns you into terror and awe. Your senses and imagination cannot grasp its immensity. Your only hope is to remove it from your terrified perception and into a conceptual category. Edgar Allan Poe's 'A Descent into the Maelstrom' (1841) contrasts the violent power of an ocean whirlpool with perspectives from which it can be intellectually mastered, while Jules Verne's *Voyages extraordinaires* (1863–1920) evoke the sublime wonders of the natural world only to catalogue and thus domesticate them.

Despite sf's claim to champion reason, pulp magazine titles betray as great a concern with sublime affects: *Amazing Stories, Astounding Stories, Startling Stories, Thrilling Wonder Stories*. Such sf produced a pleasurable 'sensawunda' through invocations of scale: in E.E. 'Doc' Smith's *Skylark* stories (1928–66), distances and velocities escalate, interstellar and intergalactic space is traversed as spaceships and weapons become ever more powerful, capable of destroying not merely planets and stars but entire galaxies; his *Lensman* stories (1937–54), recounting the closing centuries of a two-billion-year conflict, were modestly known as *The History of Civilization*.

Sf produced a pleasurable 'sensawunda'

Sf also sometimes produces a sensawunda through a closing line whose implications radically change our understanding of the preceding story. For example, Arthur C. Clarke's 'The Nine Billion Names of God' (1953) concludes with 'Overhead, without any fuss, the stars were going out'. *The Signal* (Eubank 2014) is structured by a series of similar reframings that build to an even more unexpected, fleetingly glimpsed climactic revelation.

Initially, cinema was primarily organised around the spectacular: the mere fact of moving images; unusual views and exotic locations; staged events, from train crashes to the electrocution of an elephant; new perspectives produced by slow motion, by accelerated motion and by microscopic, telescopic and time-lapse photography; and, of course, special effects. When narrative cinema became dominant around 1907, such spectacular attractions were not abandoned but incorporated into stories.

George Méliès, director of *A Trip to the Moon* (1902), continued to disdain narrative, regarding it as a pretext for linking together the tricks he wanted to stage. Sf has never entirely rejected this logic. As Stephen Neale's *Genre* (1980) notes, sf film narratives frequently exist 'to motivate the production of special effects', typically ending either 'with the best' of them or 'the point at which they are multiplied with greatest intensity' (p.31), as in *Close Encounters of the Third Kind* (Spielberg 1977) or *Star Wars* (Lucas 1977). Sean Cubitt's *The Cinema Effect* (2004) describes perfunctory blockbuster narratives as clothes lines from which to hang spectacular sequences – which themselves often function as adverts for the technology/company that produced them and for spin-off toys and games.

Which is not to say that they cannot also evoke the sublime: the Krell machines stretching down into the core of the *Forbidden Planet* (Wilcox 1956); the psychedelic trip into infinity of *2001: A Space Odyssey* (Kubrick 1968); the fractally detailed Los Angeles of *Blade Runner* (Scott 1982); the grotesque roiling flesh of *The Thing* (Carpenter 1982).

The sf of scale

- Elizabeth Bear, *Ancestral Night* (2018)
- Cixin Liu, *The Three-Body Problem* (2008)*
- Alastair Reynolds, *Revelation Space* (2000)*
- Stephen Baxter, the *Xeelee* sequence (1987–)
- Olaf Stapledon, *Starmaker* (1937)

Spectacular visions

- *Gravity* (Cuarón 2013)
- *Avatar* (Cameron 2009)*
- *Brainstorm* (Trumbull 1983)
- *Fantastic Voyage* (Fleischer 1966)
- *Road to the Stars* (Klushantsev 1957)

Two

HISTORY

MARK BOULD

Discovering our place in the universe, in time and among species.

The emergence of sf can be linked to three particular scientific revolutions, which dislodged humans from the centre of the universe, reduced human history to a tiny fraction of geological time and established that humans were just one species among many, all subject to biological and environmental determinants.

In 1543, Nicolaus Copernicus, drawing on carefully collated scientific data, challenged the Ptolemaic model of the solar system endorsed by the Catholic Church. Rather than the Earth being central, orbited by the Sun and the five known planets, Copernicus showed that the Sun was central and the Earth one of the six planets orbiting it. In 1609, Johannes Kepler refined this heliocentric model, demonstrating that planetary orbits were elliptical, not circular. In 1632, the Inquisition forced Galileo Galilei to recant his support of Copernicus, but by the end of the century, Isaac Newton's laws of motion and gravitation established heliocentrism beyond any doubt.

This Copernican revolution opened up the cosmos to all kinds of speculation. Over two hundred interplanetary romances appeared during the seventeenth century, many of them wrestling with the possibility of alien life – and whether aliens are sinless or, like humankind, fallen. C.S. Lewis' *Out of the Silent Planet* (1938),* James Blish's *A Case of Conscience* (1958)* and Mary Doria Russell's *The Sparrow* (1996)* return to such theological questions, while science-fiction-alised historical novels such as Neal Stephenson's *Quicksilver* (2003)* and Kim Stanley Robinson's *Galileo's Dream* (2009) reconstruct the turmoil of the period. Robert A. Heinlein's 'Universe' (1941) reworks the Copernican revolution on board a massive starship where the descendants of the crew have forgotten their mission and the true nature of their surroundings. The protagonist argues

> **This Copernican revolution opened up the cosmos to all kinds of speculation and unlocked the temporal imagination**

that there is an Outside through which the ship travels, and at his ensuing trial for heresy echoes the recanting Galileo's muttered 'And yet it moves'. Greg Egan's *Incandescence* (2008) is rather more elaborate: insect-like aliens living inside a worldlet orbiting within the accretion disc of a collapsed star must develop, from the most basic of initial observations, an understanding of gravitation, orbital dynamics and general relativity in order not only to comprehend but also to save their habitat.

The Copernican revolution also unlocked the temporal imagination. While the Protestant Archbishop James Usher asserted in 1650 that, according to Biblical genealogies, the Earth was created in 4004 BCE, less than a century later, the French diplomat and natural historian Benoît de Maillet calculated from geological and other evidence that the Earth was over two billion years old and that land animals had evolved from sea creatures. Although his reasoning was faulty, de Maillet anticipated the next two revolutions. The first, associated with Charles Lyell's *Principles of Geology* (1830–33), demonstrated the much greater age of the Earth; the second, associated with Charles Darwin's *On the Origin of Species* (1859), established the theory of evolution.

Because of the timescales involved, and because most of the time nothing is visibly happening, geology and evolution are difficult to turn into stories. Jules Verne's *A Journey to the Centre of the Earth* (1864) spatialises time, its protagonists descending through the Earth's crust, and thus through the fossil record, until in a deep cavern they encounter dinosaurs and a pre-human figure. Such isolated pockets of prehistoric time survive into the present in Arthur Conan Doyle's *The Lost World* (1912) and Vladimir A. Obruchev's *Plutonia* (1915); or prehistory itself is accessed by time travellers, as in Ray Bradbury's 'A Sound of Thunder' (1952) and L. Sprague de Camp's 'A Gun for Dinosaur'

Machine evolution

- Martha Wells, *Network Effect* (2020)*
- Daniel H. Wilson, *Robopocalypse* (2011)*
- Ted Chiang, *The Life Cycle of Software Objects* (2010)
- Greg Egan, *Diaspora* (1997)
- Richard Powers, *Galatea 2.2* (1995)

(1956).* Stephen Baxter's *Evolution* (2002) traces genetic descendants of a mammal that survived the K-T asteroid impact 65 million years ago. Recording geological and climatological upheavals, each section focuses on a representative example of a different successor species, including contemporary Homo sapiens; it culminates 500 million years in the future, with the last monkey-like posthumans, who live in symbiosis with trees, driven to extinction by environmental changes.

A common mode of examining evolutionary change involves confrontations with or between primates, hominids and humans, with varying degrees of attention to palaeontological, archae-ological and anthropological science. In J.H. Rosney aîné's *Quest for Fire* (1911), Neanderthals struggle against various not-quite-humans, including xenophobic pigmies and cannibals, while in J. Leslie Mitchell's *Three Go Back* (1932), time travellers get caught up in the struggle between proto-Basques and savage Neanderthals. In William Golding's *The Inheritors* (1955), Neanderthals witness the rise of Cro-Magnons, while Roy Lewis' comically anachronistic *The Evolution Man* (1960) depicts recent-ly-down-from-the-trees Pleistocene characters with distinctly suburban attitudes and a painful awareness of how far they still have to go in the evolutionary and cultural development of humankind. In Jean M. Auel's *The Clan of the Cave Bear* (1980),* an orphaned Cro-Magnon is raised by Neanderthals, while the protagonist of Michael Bishop's *No Enemy But Time* (1982) travels back in time to live among Homo habilis. Doris Lessing's *The Cleft* (2007) imagines a secret prehistory of humanity in which an all-female species, which reproduces asexually, suddenly start giving birth to male children. Kim Stanley Robinson's *Shaman* (2013) depicts the life of early modern humans during the last ice age, including friendship with Neanderthals.

Sf sometimes attempts to generate the affect of a scientific revolution through a rhetorically heightened moment of concep-tual breakthrough, when the protagonist – and the reader or viewer – suddenly realises that the world of the story is radically different from what they had previously supposed it to be. In Isaac Asimov's 'Nightfall' (1941), the planet Lagash orbits one of three closely packed pairs of binary stars. Archaeologists have discovered evidence of nine previous civilisations, each of which was destroyed in a planet-wide conflagration when, every 2049 years, five of the stars are below the horizon and the sixth is eclipsed. Astronomers believe that the sudden plunge into absolute darkness drives Lagashians to civilisation-destroying madness – that is, until the dazzling revelation of thirty thousand stars in the night sky. In Heinlein's 'Universe', the conceptual breakthrough is a rather pedestrian midway plot point, but for Asimov it is a climactic rupture that cannot be easily assimilated.

Such moments are also found in Frederik Pohl's 'The Tunnel under the World' (1955) and *Dark City* (Proyas 1998), in each of which reality turns out to be a simulation. Philip K. Dick's *Do Androids Dream of Electric Sheep?* (1968) rapidly concatenates such revelations, repeatedly pulling the rug out from under the reader.

→	**Colonialism and imperialism**

MARK BOULD

Sf is a child of colonialism. But an increasingly rebellious one.

Colonialism in the modern world began with the fifteenth- and sixteenth-century European 'voyages of discovery' and the ensuing overseas commercial ventures of Britain, France, Holland, Portugal and Spain that, along with the Dutch and British agricultural revolutions, gave rise to capitalism as a world-system. With murderous vigour, these European powers seized land in the Americas, extracted natural resources and labour power, killed 50 million Indigenous people in 150 years, enslaved and transported 15 million West and Central Africans to the Americas (one-sixth died en route) and enslaved their descendants.

The plantation colonialism of the Caribbean sugar trade brought relatively few European migrants, but settler colonialism in the US and Canada, for example, involved mass migration, the genocidal displacement of Indigenous populations and the annexations of Hawai'i, Louisiana, Puerto Rico and Texas. In contrast, the Indian subcontinent was subject to administrative colonialism, in which a small number of Britons, aided by a local comprador class, controlled the country through a bureaucratic, economic and military apparatus.

Colonialism violently restructured the entire world for the colonisers' benefit

Colonialism violently restructured the entire world for the colonisers' benefit. It wiped out populations and destroyed cultures, lifeways and ecosystems. It reordered colonised societies and economies, permanently subordinating them to the colonisers' interests. At the same time, colonising nations stripped their own populations of the means of subsistence, forcibly integrating them into labour markets.

Colonialism can be understood as a specific historical phase in an ongoing imperial project to expand commerce within particular political and legal frameworks that, backed by military force, posture as neutral but tilt heavily in the colonisers' favour. As the capitalist economic system more fully penetrated the world, colonisers no longer needed direct control of colonies. From the outset, the hard-won independence of the new post-colonies was compromised, inextricably bound up in the neocolonialist world-system perpetuating colonial hierarchies. New forms of imperialism crystallised, such as the global power exerted by the US through its enormous military and economic influence, and by its key contemporary rivals, the EU and the BRIC(S) nations. Nowadays, 'Empire' often refers not to nation-states exercising power but to the globalised networks of domination and subordination in which they operate.

All of this shaped sf.

In *Frankenstein* (1818), Mary Shelley's creature imagines life with his mate in a naturally bountiful and apparently unpopulated South America. This fantasy of empty lands is central to colonialism, as is the conviction that any natural resources not being used 'properly' by Indigenous people are free for the taking. Acquisition, accumulation and incorporation underpin Daniel Defoe's *Robinson Crusoe* (1719) and sf from Jules Verne's *The Mysterious Island* (1875) onwards, but not always uncritically. For example, in suffragist Inez Haynes Gillmore's *Angel Island* (1914), when shipwrecked men discover flying women, their various qualms about capturing them, cutting off their wings and forcing them into marriage are ultimately just a civilised veneer over the patriarchal-colonial drive to own and control.

The voyage to a different society often estranges the homeland. In Jonathan Swift's *Gulliver's Travels* (1726), Gulliver is so upset by the Houyhnhnms, ultra-rational equine creatures who dominate savage human-like Yahoos, that on his return to England, he can see his countrymen only as irrational beasts. In H.G. Wells' subjection of southern England to overwhelming Martian force in *The War of the Worlds* (1898), anti-colonial

Hearts of darkness

- Joanna Sinisalo, *Birdbrain* (2008)
- Lucius Shepard, *Life during Wartime* (1987)
- Robert Silverberg, *Downward to the Earth* (1970)
- J.G. Ballard, *The Crystal World* (1966)
- Jack London, 'The Red One' (1918)

Anti-colonial sf

- Basma Ghalayini, ed., *Palestine + 100* (2019)
- John A. Williams, *The Man Who Cried I Am* (1967)
- Karel Čapek, *War with the Newts* (1936)
- George S. Schuyler, *Black Empire* (1936–38)
- W.E.B. DuBois, *Dark Princess* (1928)

Lost worlds

- Pierre Benoit, *L'Atlantide* (1919)
- Francis Stevens, *The Citadel of Fear* (1918)
- Edgar Rice Burroughs, *At the Earth's Core* (1914)
- James De Mille, *A Strange Manuscript Found in a Copper Cylinder* (1888)
- H. Rider Haggard, *She* (1887)

sentiments collide with colonial ideology. He likens the situation to the British genocide in Tasmania, but describes Tasmanians as a stone-age leftover whose unsuitedness to the modern world made their end inevitable. Although the Martians are effectively more evolved humans, he cannot let them destroy us. In Garrett P. Serviss' unofficial sequel, *Edison's Conquest of Mars* (1898), a terrestrial fleet of avenging spaceships commits genocide without compunction. It is just Manifest Destiny in space. Sf often reformulated this kind of American exceptionalism as human exceptionalism – *Astounding* editor John W. Campbell would not countenance aliens defeating humans – but it was only ever thinly disguised white supremacism.

Lost race tales made up roughly 10 percent of Anglophone sf before the specialist pulps. Such stories reproduce the racialised myth of progress in which Indigenous people are primitive, if occasionally noble, and incapable of building civilisations. They are designated 'good' or 'bad' natives entirely in terms of how they serve European interlopers' interests. Frequently, the lost race is descended from classical Europe (or Atlantis), thus granting the European explorer miscegenation-free romance with a 'white' queen, priestess or serving girl, even as he defeats a nefarious priest or adviser, thus 'liberating' the natives from superstition and oppression. However, the rediscovered civilisation is typically lost again, forever unintegrated into the world-system except as a source of primitive accumulation, such as the diamonds with which explorers return from H. Rider Haggard's *King Solomon's Mines* (1885), Arthur Conan Doyle's *The Lost World* (1912) and Michael Crichton's *Congo* (1980). Elements of lost-race tales and other colonial adventure fiction persist: for example, the contemporary zombie film typically reworks the narratives of settlers travelling through hostile territory or besieged by Indigenous people.

Colonialism insists it is benevolent: the Federation, not the Borg. In the post-apocalyptic conclusion to *Things to Come* (Menzies 1936), civilisation re-establishes itself in the form of the Wings Over the World organisation. Based in Basra, and uninterested in 'nations', 'flags' or 'folly', it reaches out to unite the remnants of humanity. But it is an imperial project intent on 'tearing out the wealth of this planet', establishing the framework of 'law . . . order and trade' and backing it up with the threat of military force: an aerial armada, with gas bombs and black-clad paratroopers, is always on hand.

When Western sf does critique the homeland, it typically does so from the position of a notional rather than actual outsider, but nonetheless it does sometimes articulate something of the colonised's experience. For example, in Sonya Dorman's 'When I Was Miss Dow' (1966) as the sexless shape-shifting alien protagonist must adopt human – and female – form to investigate the men colonising her planet, its feminist critique of patriarchy subordinates but does not subsume its anti-colonial perspective. But when that criticism comes from those who have survived the apocalypse of colonialism and who live under neocolonialism, it is often harrowing, as in Octavia E. Butler's 'Bloodchild' (1984), which painfully renders the grotesque impossibility of living enslaved and in the aftermath of slavery.

MARK BOULD

Sf has many points of origin, not all of them in English.

The term *roman scientifique* was coined in the 1750s to describe fanciful scientific ideas, and in the 1880s it was applied to Émile Zola's naturalist novels about the shaping of character by heredity and environment. It was also one of several competing terms – *roman futuriste, fantaisies scientifiques, voyages imaginaires, mondes imaginaires, le merveilleux scientifique* – for an emerging form of fiction that only really coalesced into a self-conscious genre in the 1870s. Its roots, however, can be traced back to the collision of older forms – the marvellous, the travellers' tale – with the new understandings of the world arising from colonial expansion and natural philosophy (science). Speculations about the status of humans in the universe and the possibility of life on other planets often came into conflict with the Catholic church and state. Rabelais' *Gargantua and Pantagruel* (1532–52), Cyrano de Bergerac's *Other Worlds* (1657, 1662) and Voltaire's *Micromégas* (1752) explore such philosophical, scientific and political ideas through alien visitors, extraterrestrial civilisations and comedy, which also help to deflect charges of blasphemy and dissent.

Popularising – and imaginatively riffing on – scientific ideas and worldviews

Philosophical tales and carnivalesque satires proliferated and, as ideologies of material progress developed, began to imagine futures radically different to the present, as in Louis-Sébastien Mercier's *Memoirs of the Year Two Thousand Five Hundred* (1777) and Félix Bodin's *The Novel of the Future* (1834). This typically led to apocalyptic, utopian or dystopian visions, as in, respectively, Jean-Baptiste Cousin de Grainville's *The Last Man* (1805), Étienne Cabet's *Travels in Icaria* (1839) and Émile Souvestre's *The World as It Shall Be* (1846).

The possibilities of the roman scientifique appealed to political radicals, as demonstrated by feminist Communard

Louise Michel's *The Human Microbes* (1886),* socialist Alain le Drimeur's *The Future City* (1890), anarchist Jules Lermina's *Mysteryville* (1904–5) and communist Anatole France's *The White Stone* (1905). However, the key writers were more preoccupied with popularising – and imaginatively riffing on – scientific ideas and worldviews. There were two broad tendencies: the Flammarionesque and the Vernian.

Camille Flammarion's *Lumen* (1872) argues that humans – and an array of aliens – derive our forms not from God but from material circumstances. In his far-future *Omega: The Last Days of the World* (1883), the Sun dies and the Earth freezes. J.-H. Rosny aîné was also devoted to visionary speculations: in 'The Xipehuz' (1887), prehistoric humans face an invasion of incomprehensible aliens; in 'The Cataclysm' (1887), a hill-sized chunk of extraterrestrial matter exercises a peculiar influence on its surroundings, including humans; and 'Another World' (1895) reveals the entities, invisible to human eyes, with which we share the planet. Maurice Renard's *The Blue Peril* (1911) successfully incorporates such weird elements into a more conventional adventure narrative.

Despite taking readers *From the Earth to the Moon* (1865), *Around the Moon* (1869) and even *Off on a Comet* (1877), Jules Verne's imagination was primarily terrestrial. To explore the depths of prehistoric time, *A Journey to the Centre of the Earth* (1864) descends through the fossil record as if walking through a museum exhibit. *The Adventures of Captain Hatteras* (1864) faithfully details the northerly extremes reached by earlier polar explorers as it goes beyond them. Captain Nemo's futuristic submarine travels *Twenty Thousand Leagues under the Seas* (1870), mainly so Verne can depict ocean environments and their inhabitants. Indeed, his novels extensively recycled information gleaned from scientific, geographical and historical textbooks and reviews. They fall between two extremes: while the Moon

Roman scientifique on screen

- ☐ *The Deadly Invention* (Zeman 1958)
- ☐ *Paris qui dort* (Clair 1925)
- ☐ *The Hands of Orlac* (Wiene 1924)
- ☐ *L'Atlantide* (Feyder 1921)
- ☐ *A Trip to the Moon* (Méliès 1902)

novels focus on engineering and other practicalities, with few enlivening incidents, Around the World in Eighty Days (1873) is, despite the organisational demands of such a journey, comprised almost entirely of exciting episodes. Early English translations of his work – many still reprinted – cut much of the informational content, deforming his novels into boys' adventure stories.

Verne's influence was immediate and global. In France, it is represented by Georges Le Faure and Henri de Graffigny's The Extraordinary Adventures of a Russian Scientist across the Solar System (1888), whose blend of interplanetary adventures and science popularisation anticipates hard-sf, and by illustrator-turned-novelist Albert Robida. His globetrotting and briefly interplanetary The Adventures of Saturnin Farandoul (1879) pays explicit homage by recasting five of Verne's well-known characters, mostly as antagonists. His amiable, satirical and mildly feminist The Twentieth Century (1883)* explodes Verne's fastidious technological speculations into a fantasia of innovations and consequences, including an electrified Paris, high-speed trains, personal airships, videophones, television shopping, mass tourism and pollution. Most authors, though, preferred isolated technoscientific breakthroughs, as in Verne's Robur the Conqueror (1886)* and Villiers de l'Isle Adam's The Future Eve (1886), or to fret about industrialisation, as in Verne's The Begum's Millions (1879) and Didier de Chousy's Ignis: The Central Fire (1883).

Many romans scientifiques were feuilleton fiction, published in daily, weekly and monthly newspapers and magazines otherwise devoted to non-fiction. Novels serialised in this way – instalments rapidly improvised on short deadlines and within tight space constraints, with little opportunity for revision, and extended or curtailed as reader interest waxed or waned – struggled to incorporate complex world-building or elaborate speculation. Hence, a large number took the form of contemporary adventures stories and thrillers in which new technologies – often weapons – did little more than motivate and enable melodramatic action. Vivid examples include Gustave Le Rouge and Gustave Guitton's The Dominion of the World (1899), in which a trio of heroes take on billionaires bent on ruling the world, Le Rouge's interplanetary Vampires of Mars (1908, 1909) and Jean de La Hire's long series of novels featuring the Nyctalope, beginning with The Nyctalope on Mars (1911) – an unofficial sequel to Wells' War of the Worlds in which Flammarion makes an appearance.

World War One restricted the roman scientifique to propaganda purposes and, always fairly marginal, it limped on through the interwar years, often increasingly bleak. For example, workers revolting against brutal exploitation in Claude Farrère's *Useless Hands* (1920) are replaced with automata then slaughtered with a death ray; in Théo Varlet and Octave Joncquel's *The Martian Epic* (1921–22), invading Martians lay waste to the Earth, and the Jovians, when asked for help, respond by destroying Mars.

After World War Two, the *roman scientifique* was effectively killed off by the influx of American sf translated for the *Rayon fantastique* and *Présence du Futur* book series (French writers were more commonly published in the less prestigious *Fleuve noir* line). English translations of post-war French sf, by such authors as Pierre Barbet, René Barjavel, Serge Brussolo, Philippe Curval, Michel Jeury, Gérard Klein, Bernard Werber and Stefan Wul, remain infrequent, but thanks to a flurry of new translations, the *roman scientifique* has never been so accessible for Anglophone readers.

→ | The British scientific romance

MARK BOULD

With H.G. Wells' success, the scientific romance coalesced.

The term 'scientific romance' was coined in the 1780s to describe scientific claims that seemed preposterous and preposterous claims that were presented as scientific. This derogatory usage faded away in the mid-nineteenth century – just as some commentators on early Verne translations anglicised '*roman scientifique*'.

Throughout the nineteenth century, British fiction publishing was divided between crude penny-dreadfuls and two-penny novelettes and the costly three-decker novels favoured by circulating libraries; from around 1850, cheaper 'railway novels' – usually belated reprints – filled the middle ground. However, in the 1890s, mass literacy (thanks to education reforms in the 1870s and 1880s) and new linotype machines (which made printing quicker) saw new venues for short and long fiction proliferate, exemplified by *The Strand* (1891–1950). The market for affordable books also expanded – and effectively killed off the fiction magazines after WWI. Scientific romance, at its most popular in the late 1890s and the early 1930s, accounted for a small percentage of this fiction, but with H.G. Wells' early stories and novels, it reached sufficient critical mass to be considered a distinct tradition.

Harbingers of our potential future, harbingers of our doom

However, its roots can be found earlier, in the imaginative vistas opened up by natural philosophy, political and economic upheavals, and colonial ventures.

Thomas More's *Utopia* (1516) satirises the state of Europe (and England) before describing a voyage to an island off Brazil, where society is organised along rather different lines. The moon plays a similar role in Francis Godwin's *The Man in the Moone* (1638), Samuel Brunt's *Voyage to Cacklogalliana* (1727) and Daniel Defoe's *The Consolidator* (1705). In Jonathan Swift's earthbound *Gulliver's Travels* (1726), four voyages 'into several remote nations of the world' offer ribald fantasias on scale – extrapolated from new optical devices, the telescope and microscope – and satires on the Royal Society and excessive devotion to rationality. Margaret Cavendish's *The Blazing World* (1666) had already sounded the alarm about Enlightenment reason but was mainly concerned about it eclipsing occult philosophy's revealed 'truths' and disrupting social hierarchy.

Fascination with the esoteric runs through the scientific romance, including the apocalyptic theological fantasy of M.P. Shiel's *The Purple Cloud* (1901), the weird materialist metaphysics of William Hope Hodgson's *The House on the Borderland* (1908) and *The Night Land* (1912) and the gnostic allegory of David Lindsay's *A Voyage to Arcturus* (1920). However, the autodidactic protagonist of Mary Shelley's *Frankenstein* (1818) begins to marry arcane alchemical knowledge with modern science. He sacrifices familial and romantic attachments as he usurps the female role in reproduction, then reels horrified from his creation and loses his grip on reason. When the creature demands a mate, Frankenstein suffers a terrifying vision of their monstrous offspring returning for revenge. He destroys the partially constructed female body and devotes his life to pursuing the creature to whom he is inextricably bound. In Robert Louis Stevenson's *Strange Case of Dr Jekyll and Mr Hyde* (1886) and H.G. Wells' *The Island of Doctor Moreau* (1896) and *The Invisible Man* (1897), against similar backdrops of colonial and queer anxiety, monomaniacal derangements likewise propel the scientific endeavours that drive the scientists mad.

These novels also articulate the tension between religious and scientific worldviews foregrounded by evolutionary theory. The Vril-ya of Edward Bulwer-Lytton's *The Coming Race* (1871) are simultaneously more ancient and more advanced than humans: harbingers of our potential future, they have created

Scientific romance on screen

- *Last and First Men* (Jóhannsson 2020)
- *The Invisible Man* (Whale 1933)
- *Island of Lost Souls* (Kenton 1932)
- *Frankenstein* (Whale 1931)*
- *Dr Jekyll and Mr Hyde* (Mamoulian 1931)

a prosperous egalitarian society; harbingers of our doom, they seem destined to supplant us. In Wells' *The Time Machine* (1895), humankind evolves into two separate species, the beautiful childlike Eloi and the monstrous subterranean Morlocks, before evolving over tens of millions of years into more basic lifeforms capable of living on a dying world. Olaf Stapledon's *Last and First Men* (1930) charts the evolution of seventeen subsequent human species over two billion years. On a smaller scale, his *Odd John* (1935) – like J.D. Beresford's *The Hampdenshire Wonder* (1911) and Muriel Jaeger's *The Man with Six Senses* (1927) – ponders the fate of a more highly evolved human born into the present. Conversely, in E.V. Odle's cyborg comedy *The Clockwork Man* (1923) and Katharine Burdekin's gender-swapping *Proud Man* (1934), visitors from the future find contemporary social relations peculiar.

Evolutionarily advanced others and utopias are often defined as more rational, but authors frequently treat this quality with ambivalence: in Wells' *The First Men in the Moon* (1900–1901), there is something awful about the lunar society, which engineers its subjects to fulfil specific roles. Appalled by the American Edward Bellamy's *Looking Backward* (1888) – which imagines state and market mechanisms automatically producing an urban utopia without the need for human intervention – William Morris' *New from Nowhere* (1890) emphasises the role of human agency in creating a decentralised pastoral socialism. E.M. Forster's 'The Machine Stops' (1909) pictures technologically maintained alienation, Rose Macaulay's *What Not* (1918) mocks social engineering and Jaeger's *The Question Mark* (1926) worries whether egalitarian plenitude can produce happiness. This tendency culminates in two of the best-known dystopias, Aldous Huxley's *Brave New World* (1932) and George Orwell's *Nineteen Eighty-Four* (1949), in which reason becomes utterly irrational.

For decades, the future war story was the most popular kind of scientific romance. Initiated by George Tomkyns Chesney's *The Battle of Dorking* (1871), it relished violent inter-imperial rivalry. It became more fantastical in George Griffiths' fantasy of airborne anarchists *The Angel of the Revolution* (1893),* and was parodied and pastiched in P.G. Wodehouse's *The Swoop* (1909) and Saki's *When William Came* (1913). It is at its most science-fictional in Wells' *The War of the Worlds* (1897), which replaces imperial rivals with Martian invaders and sees colonial aggression lay waste to the centre of Empire.

But after the horrors of WWI, Edward Shanks' *The People of the Ruins* (1920), Cicely Hamilton's *Theodore Savage* (1922), John Collier's *Tom's-A-Cold* (1933), Alun Llewellyn's *Strange Invaders* (1934), Philip George Chadwick's *The Death Guard* (1939) and R.C. Sherriff's *The Hopkins Manuscript* (1939) imagine further war not only as inevitable but also as so devastating that civilisation could never recover. Anxieties about the deadly rationalisation of unreason become overtly anti-fascist in J. Leslie Mitchell's *Gay Hunter* (1934), Storm Jameson's *In the Second Year* (1936) and Burdekin's *The End of This Day's Business* (1935; published 1989) and *Swastika Night* (1937).

The scientific romance did not really re-emerge after the Second World War. Derailed by the 1950s 'mushroom boom' of cheap lurid genre paperbacks, it was transformed by the influence of maturing American magazine sf. But scientific romance's distinctive tone – sceptical, frustrated, melancholic, post-imperial – can still be heard in British sf.

MARK BOULD

Expansion, genocide, innovation and unreason – American style.

After the War of Independence (1775–83), the thirteen heavily indebted European colonies on the Eastern seaboard began over a century of genocidal expansion, with the last few western territories (bar Alaska) becoming states by 1912. In this long nineteenth century, stolen land and resources provided the raw materials, and African American chattel slavery much of the labour, on which this new nation's wealth was built. At the same time, mass immigration, primarily from Europe, spurred a huge growth in population, from around 5 million to over 75 million. Although the period of westward expansion is generally imagined in terms of wilderness, isolated ranches, small settlements and agriculture, the urban population rose from fewer than 500,000 to over 30 million (i.e., from 5 percent to 40 percent of the total population). It was a century of almost constant warfare, primarily against Native American Indian nations, but also against North African nations, Britain, Mexico, China, Canada, Korea, Samoa, Germany, Spain and the Philippines, and of civil war between Northern and Southern states. It was also an era of technological marvels: American innovations included chain suspension bridges, combine harvesters, steam shovels, vulcanised rubber, jack hammers, escalators, vacuum cleaners, repeating rifles, machine guns, steam-powered motorcycles, barbed wire, ticker tape, transcontinental railroads, sandblasting, mimeographs, phonographs, thermostats, skyscrapers, photographic film and the electric chair.

A century of almost constant warfare and an era of technological marvels

Dime-novel sf, such as Edward S. Ellis' *The Steam Man of the Prairies* (1868), Harry Enton's *Frank Reade and His Steam Man of the Plains* (1876)* and Luis P. Senarens' 174 *Franke Reade, Jr* (1882–99) and 103 *Jack Wright* (1891–96) titles, celebrate colonial conquest and new technologies. These boy-inventor stories typically involve a new device, often a mode of transport, along with total commitment to capitalism, 'progress' and violent, often genocidal, action against racial others.

Similar material underpinned much of the sf that appeared in the general fiction pulps. For example, *The Argosy* (1882–1979), *The All-Story* (1905–20) and *Blue Book* (1905–56) published fiction by Ray Cummings, George Allan England, Garrett P. Serviss, Murray Leinster, A. Merritt and Philip Wylie, but the most influential of these stories was Edgar Rice Burroughs' *A Princess of Mars* (1912).* It starts as a Wild West adventure in Arizona, but becomes a planetary romance. Fleeing Apaches, gold-prospecting Confederate veteran John Carter is mysteriously transported to Mars. On the dying desert world, where ancient civilisations deploy superscience technologies, his martial prowess elevates him through the ranks of the nomadic warlike six-armed green Martians. He then rescues a beautiful humanoid red Martian princess, falls in love, becomes a prince and saves the planet. Burroughs wrote ten sequels and prompted countless imitations; his other sf includes *Beyond Thirty* (1915), *The Land That Time Forgot* (1918) and *Pirates of Venus* (1932).*

Lowbrow popular fiction was not American sf's only root. Until the late nineteenth century, American literature was dominated not by realism but by romance forms. Charles Brockden Brown's gothic *Wieland* (1798) teems with strange and potentially supernatural events, all of which are eventually explained away through spontaneous combustion, religious mania and ventriloquism. This rationalisation of the fantastic is central to Edgar Allan Poe's work. The satirical 'The Unparalleled Adventure of Hans Pfall' (1835) turns into an account of a lunar voyage full of scientific observations, calculations and hypotheses. *The Narrative of Arthur Gordon Pym* (1838) borrows realistic details from accounts of actual voyages, which helps to make more credible its several

---

Sf from the general pulps

- ◘ Edwin Balmer and Philip Wylie, *When Worlds Collide* (1932–33)*
- ◘ Ray Cummings, *The Girl in the Golden Atom* (1919–20)
- ◘ Francis Stevens, *The Heads of Cerberus* (1919)
- ◘ A. Merritt, *The Moon Pool* (1918–19)
- ◘ George Allan England, *Darkness and Dawn* (1912–13)

weird and gruesome interludes and its climactic encounter with sublime alterity. Later stories, such as 'The Facts in the Case of M. Valdemar' (1845), smoothly blend the charismatic authority of technical terminology with more conventional techniques of narrative verisimilitude.

While Poe laid the rhetorical groundwork for what would become hard-sf, the gothic nonetheless persisted. Hypnosis and other modes of psychological manipulation are central to Nathaniel Hawthorne's early novels, but 'The Birthmark' (1843), 'The Artist of the Beautiful' (1844) and 'Rappaccini's Daughter' (1844) are more fully science-fictional explorations of the (masculinist) psychology of scientists, mechanics and experimenters. Herman Melville's 'The Bell-Tower' (1855) likewise features a Byronic obsessive, an architect who creates and is killed by an automaton.

Automata also turn on their makers in Fitz James O'Brien's 'The Wondersmith' (1859) and Ambrose Bierce's 'Moxon's Master' (1899). In O'Brien's 'The Diamond Lens' (1858), the very device through which its inventor observes the otherwise invisible microscopic world contained in a drop of water destroys the object of its gaze. Mark Twain's *A Connecticut Yankee in King Arthur's Court* (1889) culminates in an even bleaker view of technology. When Hank Morgan timeslips back to Camelot, his Yankee knowhow, rationality and democratic aversion to feudalism elevate him to Arthur's right hand, but his sense of superiority is undermined by the slaughter his 'invention' of electric fences, Gatling guns and explosives unleashes.

Realistic details borrowed from accounts of actual voyages help to make more credible its several weird and gruesome interludes and its climactic encounter with sublime alterity.

In contrast, Edward Bellamy's *Looking Backward* (1888)* postulates a post-scarcity future of universal white middle-class consumerism. Often misleadingly labelled socialist, its utopia is achieved through the capitalist tendency to concentrate wealth resulting in a fully integrated monopoly that, for no discernible reason, turns benevolent. African Americans, absent from this future Boston, enjoy a separate but equal existence in their own cities, the sequel explains.

Bellamy's bestseller led to an explosion of utopian fiction, including William Dean Howells' rather gently Christian socialist *A Traveler from Altruria* (1892–93)* and Jack London's *The Iron Heel* (1908), which depicts the brutal suppression of a socialist mass movement. Anti-capitalism underpins Ignatius Donnelly's bleak

Caesar's Column (1890), Upton Sinclair's comic *The Millennium* (1914) and Sinclair Lewis' anti-fascist *It Can't Happen Here* (1935). Feminist utopias include Mary Griffith's *Three Hundred Years Hence* (1836), Mary E. Bradley Lane's *Mizora* (1880–81) and Charlotte Perkins Gilman's *Herland* (1915).* Lane's and Gilman's all-female societies featured parthenogenesis but also, unfortunately, eugenics.

Early African American sf

- George Schuyler, *Black No More* (1931)
- W.E.B. Du Bois, 'The Comet' (1920)
- Roger Sherman Tracy, *The White Man's Burden* (1915)
- Pauline Hopkins, *Of One Blood* (1903)
- Sutton E. Griggs, *Imperium in Imperio* (1899)

Mad science and superscience onscreen

- *The Invisible Ray* (Hillyer 1936)
- *Flash Gordon* (Stephani and Taylor 1936)
- *The Devil-Doll* (Browning 1936)
- *The Phantom Empire* (Brower and Eason 1935)
- *The Mysterious Island* (Hubbard 1929)

MARK BOULD

Sf's dominant paradigm: unstable, contradictory – and always challenged.

Sf was published in general fiction pulps since they first appeared in 1896. *Weird Tales* (1923–54), a specialist pulp associated with horror and sword and sorcery, also carried sf, including lost-race fiction, cosmic horror, space opera and planetary romance, such as Francis Stevens' *Sunfire* (1923), H.P. Lovecraft's 'The Call of Cthulhu' (1928), Edmond Hamilton's *Interstellar Patrol* stories (1928–30) and C.L. Moore's *Northwest Smith* stories (1933–40). But when Hugo Gernsback launched *Amazing Stories* (1926–2005), the first pulp devoted entirely to sf, he set about establishing the existence, nature and scope of 'scientifiction' by identifying it instead with Edgar Allan Poe, Jules Verne, H.G. Wells and Edward Bellamy, thus borrowing much-needed cultural capital. He called for sf to combine scientific accuracy, prophetic vision and thrilling romance, but struggled to find contributors. He relied heavily on reprints of Wells, Verne and Poe and of stories from the general pulps by Edgar Rice Burroughs, A. Merritt, Garrett P. Serviss and Murray Leinster, but did also discover Miles J. Breuer, David H. Keller, E.E. 'Doc' Smith and Jack Williamson.

A serious literature based in engineering problems and scientific possibilities

After losing control of *Amazing* in 1929, Gernsback launched four new pulps, which quickly folded or merged into *Wonder Stories* (1929–55), retitled *Thrilling Wonder Stories* when he sold it in 1936. Under David Lasser and later Charles D. Hornig, it was the leading sf pulp of the early 1930s, publishing Clark Ashton Smith and debuting Clifford D. Simak, John Wyndham, Leslie F. Stone and Stanley G. Weinbaum. *Astounding Stories* (1930–) started as an action-adventure sf pulp, but from 1933, under F. Orlin Tremaine, became more thoughtful and ambitious, pursuing fiction by Leinster, Lovecraft, Moore, 'Doc' Smith, Williamson and Weinbaum, and thus stealing *Wonder Stories*' crown. Then, from

1937, new editor John W. Campbell Jr. presided over the so-called golden age of sf.

He tweaked the magazine's design, lured Simak back to sf, recruited already-established adventure pulp writer L. Ron Hubbard and debuted Lester del Rey. Then, in 1939, he debuted A.E. van Vogt, Robert A. Heinlein and Theodore Sturgeon, published one of Isaac Asimov's first stories and launched a sister magazine, *Unknown* (1939–43), devoted to 'rational' fantasy that was sometimes, as with L. Sprague de Camp's *Lest Darkness Fall* (1939), indistinguishable from sf. Campbell developed a vision of sf as a serious literature based in engineering problems and scientific possibilities, and gathered together the coterie of authors responsible for much of the next decade's defining sf. In the pages of *Astounding*, Heinlein began to map out his *Future History* (1939–87), while Asimov generated the *I, Robot* (1941–50) stories from potential contradictions within the three laws of robotics and, in the *Foundation* trilogy (1942–53), described a secret plan to minimise the period of barbarism between the fall of one galactic civilisation and the rise of another.

In the late 1940s and early 1950s, the number of sf magazines exploded. Paperback sf, pioneered by Ballantine and Ace, who from 1952 published reprint and original novels, anthologies and collections, provided further competition. *Astounding* began to lose ground, partly because Campbell's autocratic attitude and cranky preoccupations drove authors away, and partly because his vision of sf, always marred by racism and sexism, was too constraining. For example, he never published Ray Bradbury, and of the eighty-five stories Philip K. Dick published in 1952–59, only 'Impostor' (1953) appeared in *Astounding*.

In the 1950s, the most important magazines were Anthony Boucher's *The Magazine of Fantasy and Science Fiction* (1949–) and Horace L. Gold's *Galaxy* (1950–80). *F&SF* had a broader

Astounding in the 1940s

- Jack Williamson, *The Humanoids* (1947–48)
- Clifford D. Simak, *City* (1944–51)
- Henry Kuttner and C.L. Moore, *Robots Have No Tails* (1943–48)
- Fritz Leiber, *Gather, Darkness!* (1943)
- A.E. van Vogt, *Slan* (1940)

Cold War sf

- Mordecai Roshwald, *Level 7* (1959)
- Pat Frank, *Alas, Babylon* (1959)
- Leigh Brackett, *The Long Tomorrow* (1955)
- Robert A. Heinlein, *The Puppet Masters* (1951)
- Judith Merril, *Shadow on the Hearth* (1950)

generic remit and encouraged a more literary style. It published Ward Moore's alternate history *Bring the Jubilee* (1952), Zenna Henderson's *The People* stories (1952–75) about shipwrecked aliens stranded on earth, Walter M. Miller Jr.'s post-apocalyptic *A Canticle for Leibowitz* (1955–57) and the 1959 novella version of Daniel Keyes' *Flowers for Algernon* (1966), about a man whose low intelligence is boosted to genius level but then slowly declines. Such humane fiction was typical of *F&SF* regulars, some of whom were primarily or exclusively short-story writers, including Doris Pitkin Buck, Mildred Clingerman, Avram Davidson, Damon Knight and Kit Reed.

Galaxy published a wide range of sf, including Simak's *Time and Again* (1950), a time-war story imbued with anti-Campbellian decency, the 1951 novella version of Bradbury's *Fahrenheit 451* (1953) and Asimov's detective/sf crossover *The Caves of Steel* (1953). Social and satirical sf, such as Cyril M. Kornbluth's 'The Marching Morons' (1951), Frederik Pohl's 'The Midas Plague' (1954) and their collaborative *The Space Merchants* (1952), became central to *Galaxy*, while Alfred Bester's *The Demolished Man* (1952) and Sturgeon's 'Baby Is Three' (1952), the middle section of *More Than Human* (1953), are early examples of its knowing and sometimes stylish transformation of familiar materials.

By the end of the decade, though, most of the magazines were gone. *Astounding*, renamed *Analog* in 1960, plodded on, while new editors at *F&SF* and *Galaxy* unknowingly laid some of the groundwork for what would become known as the New Wave. *Galaxy* published stories by Cordwainer Smith, Jack Vance, Robert Silverberg and Harlan Ellison; *F&SF* published Joanna Russ' debut 'No Custom Stale' (1959), Roger Zelazny's 'A Rose for Ecclesiastes' (1963) and, from the UK, imported Brian W. Aldiss' *Hothouse* (1961) and J.G. Ballard's 'The Garden of Time' (1962).

The post-Campbell *Analog*, *F&SF*, *Galaxy* and *If* (1952–74), along with Asimov's *Science Fiction* (1977–) and *Omni* (1978–1995), remained important venues, but the 1970s also saw several influential original anthology series: Knight's *Orbit* (1967–80), Terry Carr's *Universe* (1971–87) and Silverberg's *New Dimensions* (1971–81). The contents pages of their combined fifty volumes are a virtual roll call of authors who came to prominence in the 1970s (Suzy McKee Charnas, Joe Haldeman, Vonda N. McIntyre, Barry N. Malzberg, Joanna Russ, James Tiptree Jr., John Varley), the 1980s (Greg Bear, Gregory Benford, Michael Bishop, Pat Cadigan, Orson Scott Card, George Alec Effinger, William

Gibson, Pat Murphy, Kim Stanley Robinson, Pamela Sargent, Lucius Shepard, John Shirley, Bruce Sterling, Joan D. Vinge, Gene Wolfe) and the 1990s (Eleanor Arnason, Nancy Kress, Michael Swanwick, Vernor Vinge).

To trace the development of Anglophone sf in the magazines and original anthologies since the mid-1980s, Gardner Dozois' *The Year's Best Science Fiction* reprint anthologies (1984–2018) are an excellent resource.

→ The New Wave

GERRY CANAVAN

Making everything new. Leaving many things unchanged.

Like so much scholarly terminology, the New Wave is difficult to define, periodise or localise. There are multiple New Waves on both sides of the Atlantic, each building in intensity during the late 1960s and coming to a head sometime in the 1970s. But the New Wave's visionary, revisionist attitude is also part of a tendency evident throughout the genre's history, from its origins to today. In this sense, the New Wave can simultaneously be seen as something that lasted only a few years, something that is still ongoing, and even perhaps something that never really happened at all, at least not in the totalising way that after-the-fact mythmaking would have it. What the New Wave meant at the time and what it might mean now very much depends on who is speaking and what exactly they are trying to say.

The term derives from the *nouvelle vague* of French directors, including Jean-Luc Godard, François Truffaut, Eric Rohmer and Claude Chabrol, whose films, beginning in the late 1950s, revolutionised both cinema and criticism. Sf's New Wave is understood to have had a similar effect, elevating and transforming the genre as well as making it more available to lofty intellectualisation and academic study.

In Britain, the New Wave is associated with *New Worlds* (1946–70) after Michael Moorcock took over as editor in 1964, bringing a new focus on 'inner space', commodity culture, US imperialism, the sexual revolution, the media landscape, ecology, feminism countercultural politics and late-modernist/early-postmodernist experiments in style. Moorcock published J.G. Ballard's increasingly experimental short fiction, including 'You: Coma: Marilyn Monroe' (1966) and 'The Assassination of John Fitzgerald Kennedy Considered as a Downhill Motor Race' (1966), later collected in *The Atrocity Exhibition* (1970); Brian Aldiss' *Report on*

United by dissatisfaction with post-war society and mouldering genre assumptions

Probability A (1967) and the Acid-Head war stories of *Barefoot in the Head* (1969); and Moorcock's own Jerry Cornelius stories, from which he spun off *The Final Programme* (1968)* and other novels. The magazine was also an important venue for several American writers, publishing Pamela Zoline's 'The Heat Death of the Universe' (1967), Thomas M. Disch's *Camp Concentration* (1967), Norman Spinrad's *Bug Jack Barron* (1967–68), Samuel R. Delany's 'Time Considered as a Helix of Semi-Precious Stones' (1968) and Harlan Ellison's 'A Boy and His Dog' (1969). Judith Merril, whose *Year's Best SF* collections (1956–70) long privileged New Wave tendencies, introduced *New Worlds* writers to America in *England Swings SF* (1968).

In the US, Ellison edited a pair of massive original anthologies: *Dangerous Visions* (1967), often seen as a kind of manifesto for the American New Wave, featured work by such major figures as Delany, Philip K. Dick, Philip José Farmer and Roger Zelazny, as well as by Aldiss, Ballard and fellow Briton John Brunner; *Again, Dangerous Visions* (1972) included Ursula K. Le Guin's *The Word for World Is Forest*, as well as fiction by Disch, Joanna Russ, James Tiptree Jr., Kurt Vonnegut Jr. and some authors not normally associated with the New Wave (Gregory Benford, Ben Bova, Dean Koontz, Gene Wolfe).

These multiple possible and overlapping New Waves were united by dissatisfaction with post-war society and mouldering genre assumptions. 'What you hold in your hands is more than a book', Ellison's *Dangerous Visions* preface opens. 'If we are lucky, it is a revolution.' First and foremost, it was a fan revolution, rejecting publishers, editors and other fans who refused to accept sf's new, ambitious, taboo-breaking scope. However, *Dangerous Visions* contains not one but two forewords by Isaac Asimov and stories by other writers who came to prominence in the 1930s, 1940s and 1950s (Lester del Rey, Fritz Leiber, Theodore

New Wave sf
▣ Philip K. Dick, *VALIS* (1981)
▣ Joanna Russ, *We Who Are about To . . .* (1975)
▣ Barry Malzberg, *Galaxies* (1975)
▣ Samuel R. Delany, *Dhalgren* (1975)
▣ Robert Silverberg, *Dying Inside* (1972)

Sturgeon, Frederik Pohl), suggesting perhaps just how much the New Wave was above all a branding exercise.

Right or wrong, the branding stuck. Darko Suvin's *Metamorphoses of Science Fiction* (1979), arguably sf studies' foundational text, rejects the bulk of the genre as 'strictly perishable', preferring the '5 to 10 per cent . . . that is aesthetically significant: in our days . . . Le Guin, Dick, Disch, Delany, . . . Aldiss, Ballard' (1). That is, the authors in Moorcock's, Merril's and Ellison's rolodexes.

The New Wave does not name a coherent political or unified artistic movement, but a constellation of new voices, perspectives, trends and thematic preoccupations that propelled sf through the 1970s before themselves starting to feel dated and routine. Although New Wave authors did not necessarily understand themselves to be collaborators and may often have had little or no contact with each other, they collectively injected a spirit of revolutionary experimentation into sf on every register: formal, political, philosophical, spiritual. An artefact from the June 1968 issue of *Galaxy* (1950–80) offers a helpful material dividing line between this constellation and its predecessor: on facing pages, two ads listing sf authors who support or oppose the US war in Vietnam. Some pro-war authors, such as Robert A. Heinlein, John W. Campbell, Larry Niven and Marion Zimmer Bradley, remain well-known, but the (retrospectively recognisable) future of sf – including those writers most celebrated in academia – is clearly on the anti-war side.

Just as it is difficult now to encounter James Joyce, Virginia Woolf and T.S. Eliot as the modernist rebels and iconoclasts they were, so it is to imagine a history of sf that does not move through figures like Le Guin, Russ, Ballard, Delany and Dick. Much of what we now see as foundational was, in its moment, a self-consciously radical attack on what had come before.

In the early 1980s, the cyberpunk movement defined itself as the New Wave's heir and overthrower. Cyberpunks united the literary craftsmanship and hallucinogenic creativity they inherited with a new focus on the form of the computer in a world whose possibilities for transformation seemed more exhausted than ever. And they experienced the New Wave's fate: ecstatic emergence, rapid canonisation, diffusion and supplantation.

So just as the New Wave never really happened, it also never really ended. The revolution Ellison announced continues to animate the practice and study of sf, no matter how many waves and -punks have since wrestled for genre supremacy.

KATIE STONE

Sisters are doing it for themselves. And for all of us.

1970s feminist sf

- Zoë Fairbairns, *Benefits* (1979)
- Kate Wilhelm, *Where Late the Sweet Birds Sang* (1976)
- James Tiptree Jr., *Warm Worlds and Otherwise* (1975)
- Doris Piserchia, *Star Rider* (1974)
- Doris Lessing, *The Memoirs of a Survivor* (1974)

In 1975, the fanzine *Khatru* published a symposium on women in sf. Over seven months, the contributors – including Ursula K. Le Guin, Joanna Russ, Samuel R. Delany and Vonda N. McIntyre, authors of, respectively, *The Left Hand of Darkness* (1969), *The Female Man* (1975), *Triton* (1976) and *Dreamsnake* (1978) – exchanged thoughtful, funny and impassioned correspondence on topics ranging from misogyny in sf publishing to feminist revolution. The conversation was driven by a shared need to acknowledge sf's active hostility to women. While some earlier female writers such as Andre Norton, Zenna Henderson and Leigh Brackett had enjoyed success, as late as 1973 the Science Fiction Writers of America's membership included just two women for every eleven men. And yet, this symposium appeared at a moment of change, on the brink of a wave of feminist writing that would alter sf forever. Alongside their letters, the contributors exchanged copies of Russ' and Delany's new novels – feminist utopias now synonymous with 1970s sf – and as they were debating the value of women-only anthologies, Pamela Sargent was editing the first of three *Women of Wonder* (1974)* reprint collections of female-authored sf.

A wave of feminist writing that would alter sf forever

This wave did not emerge from nowhere. During the 1960s, submissive Martian housewives and devilish alien queens were replaced by the sexually liberated spacefarers of Naomi Mitchison's *Memoirs of a Spacewoman* (1962) and Roger Vadim's *Barbarella* (1968). Lacking the explicitly revolutionary content of later feminist sf, they nonetheless challenged the ubiquitous image of the space*man* and foreshadowed later feminist interventions.

An earlier and more troubling precursor can be found in the proliferation of female separatist utopias at the turn of the nineteenth century, such as Charlotte Perkins Gilman's *Herland* (1915).* Featuring societies free from gendered oppression, they paved the way for Monique Wittig's *Les Guerilleres* (1969) and Suzy McKee Charnas' *Motherlines* (1978).* However, the freedoms enjoyed by Gilman's Herlanders depended upon the elimination of 'undesirable' traits from their bloodline and upon strictly policed borders. Predicated on a eugenicist understanding of reproduction, this form of feminism left no room in utopia for women of colour, working-class, queer, trans and disabled women.

Feminist sf writers of the 1970s struggled against this legacy with varying degrees of commitment and success, often replicating the racism of Gilman and her contemporaries but also finding ways to envision freer worlds. As Tom Moylan argues, they produced 'critical utopias' in direct conversation with the revolutionary protest movements for civil rights, decolonisation and women's liberation. The *Khatru* symposium repeatedly refers to consciousness-raising groups, Shulamith Firestone's Marxist feminism and the movement against the Vietnam War. These authors were not only concerned with *imagining* more utopian worlds but with bringing those worlds off the page and into existence. As Marge Piercy, author of *Woman on the Edge of Time* (1976), wrote of her fellow feminist sf creators, 'we wanted to make a better world, and in some ways, we did' (Moylan xii).

More women of wonder

- Lisa Yaszek, ed., *The Future Is Female!* (2018)*
- Lisa Yaszek and Patrick B. Sharp, eds., *Sisters of Tomorrow* (2016)
- Kristine Kathryn Rusch, ed., *Women of Futures Past* (2016)
- Ann and Jeff VanderMeer, eds., *Sisters of the Revolution* (2015)
- Alex Dally MacFarlane, ed., *The Mammoth Book of SF Stories by Women* (2014)

SARAH LOHMANN

An unsustainable world. The necessity of change.

Sf has long engaged with ecology, exploring vast geological timescales in H.G. Wells' *The Time Machine* (1895) and environments engineered to better serve human needs in Begum Rokeya's *Sultana's Dream* (1905). However, in the mid-twentieth century, sf began to focus on how humans might negatively impact the planet. A natural catastrophe floods the world in S. Fowler Wright's *Deluge* (1928), but humanity causes the crop death in John Christopher's *The Death of Grass* (1956) and the extreme climatological upheaval that threatens planetary survival in J.G. Ballard's *The Drought* (1964). While showcasing human interdependence with their environment, such novels tend to be anthropocentric, focusing more on human responses than on the ecological disaster itself.

In the later 1960s and 1970s, a more immediate interest in sustainability and ecology followed the publication of Rachel Carson's *Silent Spring* (1962), a damning indictment of pesticide use, and the Club of Rome's *Limits to Growth* (1972), which modelled the catastrophic consequences of unrestrained growth of industrialisation, population, food production, pollution and consumption of non-renewable resources. Sf responded with characteristic fervour. John Brunner's *The Sheep Look Up* (1972) critiques the way capitalism produces and profits from environmental degradation, while his *Stand on Zanzibar* (1968) explores the dangers and misery of overpopulation. Ernest Callenbach's utopian *Ecotopia* (1975), featuring the journalistic reports and personal diaries of William Weston, first US visitor to the now-independent Pacific Northwest, is more positive but also more polemical. The post-capitalist, environmentally sustainable *Ecotopia* prioritises humans over labour and rejects patriarchy. However, racial and ethnic minorities live in separate cities, male

> **The catastrophic consequences of unrestrained growth, pollution and consumption**

sexuality is identified with violence in 'war games' and there is an oddly sexist voyeurism towards female sexuality. Moreover, the main ecological and political goal of the Ecotopians is the production and maintenance of a stable system, which leaves no room for flexibility or change.

Other ecologically minded sf from the period, less optimistic and less polemical, prioritises dynamic adaptability. Naomi Mitchison's *Memoirs of a Spacewoman* (1962) centralises egalitarian, flexible and non-invasive knowledge accumulation and cooperation with non-human animals on Earth and other planets, thus showcasing a sustainable form of feminist environmental science as 'partnership not domination' (Donawerth 535). The utopian environments of Marge Piercy's *Woman on the Edge of Time* (1976) and Joanna Russ' *The Female Man* (1975) are holistic and dynamically sustainable; they allow one to 'think beyond deeply embedded frameworks for conceiving of social/natural relationships' (Garforth 397).

More recently, Eric Otto's *Green Speculations* (2012) and Amitav Ghosh's *The Great Derangement* (2016) have questioned whether the fantastical nature of sf is suited to spearheading environmental awareness. However, their fear is misguided: if we can creatively explore and learn from environmental relations and possible ecological devastation in the one genre that is intimately tied to our own reality through extrapolation, then we can also imagine better ways forward.

Ecological sf

- Sherri S. Tepper, *Grass* (1989)*
- Joan Slonczewski, *A Door into Ocean* (1986)*
- Ursula K. Le Guin, *Always Coming Home* (1985)
- Frank Herbert, *Dune* (1965)
- George R. Stewart, *Earth Abides* (1949)

Ecological screen sf

- *Nausicaä of the Valley of the Wind* (Miyazaki 1984)
- *Long Weekend* (Eggleston 1978)
- *Soylent Green* (Fleischer 1973)
- *Silent Running* (Trumbull 1972)
- *Doomwatch* (1970–72)

MARK BOULD

Sf has always been global. We just weren't paying attention.

Jules Verne and H.G. Wells enjoyed massive worldwide popularity, influencing many national and linguistic traditions other than their own. For example, *Sannikov's Land* (1926), the Russian Vladimir A. Obruchev's geological and palaeontological adventure for younger readers, is modelled on Verne, and Wells' *The Time Machine* (1895) prompted such French responses as Alfred Jarry's 'How to Construct a Time Machine' (1899), Albert Robida's *The Clock of the Centuries* (1902) and Theo Varlet and André Blandin's *Timeslip Troopers* (1923). The Soviet Yevgeny Zamyatin, responsible for a twelve-volume Russian edition of Wells (1924–26), saw his dystopian *We* (written 1920–21) translated into English (1924), Czech (1927) and French (1929); Russian-language editions appeared in Czechoslovakia (1927) and the US (1952), but in the USSR it circulated only in samizdat until 1988. Inspired by Wells' *When the Sleeper Wakes* (1899), *We* influenced Aldous Huxley's *Brave New World* (1932) and George Orwell's *Nineteen Eighty-Four* (1949).

> **The explosion of Indigenous futurisms and African sf enables us to see sf anew**

However, while translations of Anglophone sf are not uncommon, translations of sf into English remain relatively rare. Indeed, the Polish Stanisław Lem and the Soviet Arkady and Boris Strugatsky are the only foreign-language sf writers since Verne to enjoy more-or-less systematic and contemporaneous translation into English.

More recently, crowdfunding and the digital technologies underpinning ebooks and print-on-demand have enabled small presses and enthusiasts to overcome some of the constraints on publishing translations and sf from around the world. Subsequently, traditional publishers have ventured into the market. For example, Lavie Tidhar established *The World SF Blog* to support publication of *The Apex Book of World SF* (2009).*

By 2018, five volumes, the first three edited by Tidhar, had been issued by the publishing offshoot of the subscription sf webzine *Apex* (2005–). In contrast, Tidhar's more recent *The Best of World SF: Volume 1* (2020) appeared from a Bloomsbury imprint.

Small presses were also responsible for original anthologies such as Nalo Hopkinson and Uppinder Mehan's *So Long Been Dreaming* (2004) and Fabio Fernandes and Djibil al-Ayad's crowdfunded *We See a Different Frontier* (2013), and for Bill Campbell's massive crowdfunded mostly-reprints anthology *Sunspot Jungle* (2018), while traditional publishers issued Ken Liu's two volumes of *Contemporary Chinese Science Fiction in Translation* (2016, 2019) and Tarun Saint's *The Gollancz Book of South Asian Science Fiction* (2019).

A distinction is sometimes made between world literature (everything published) and World Literature (the 'best' of everything published). The 'best' usually denotes works that 'transcend' local/national circumstances to address the 'universal' human condition, but they might be better described as works from outside of Europe and the US that can be readily understood by publishers in New York, London and Paris and that cater to the white middle-class taste formations they tend to uncritically privilege and reproduce. The same undoubtedly applies to the selections from world sf that appear in the US and UK.

The Warwick Research Collective's *Combined and Uneven Development* (2015) urges us not to settle for a World Literature that ends up reproducing Eurocentrism but to instead seek out 'world-literature' – works that, regardless of their supposed quality, register the radically uneven world-system of capitalist modernity. For a similar 'world-sf', we might first look to two of the twenty-first century's most exciting sf developments: the explosion of Indigenous futurisms and African sf.

World Literature as World Sf?

- Adolfo Bioy Casares, *The Invention of Morel* (1940)
- Lao She, *Cat Country* (1933)
- Virginia Woolf, *Orlando* (1928)
- Mikhail Bulgakov, *Heart of a Dog* (1925)
- Raymond Roussel, *Locus Solus* (1914)

Indigenous futurisms

- Joshua Whitehead, ed., *Love after the End* (2020)
- Louise Erdrich, *Future Home of the Living God* (2017)
- Cherie Dimaline, *The Marrow Thieves* (2017)*
- Claire G. Coleman, *Terra Nullius* (2017)
- Lee Maracle, *Celia's Song* (2014)*

Africanfuturism/ Africanjujuism then

- Ben Okri, *The Famished Road* (1991)*
- Kojo Laing, *Woman of the Aeroplanes* (1988)
- Buchi Emecheta, *The Rape of Shavi* (1983)
- Amos Tutuola, *The Palm-Wine Drinkard* (1952)
- D.O. Fagunwa, *Forest of a Thousand Daemons* (1939)

Africanfuturism/ Africanjujuism now

- Nnedi Okorafor, *Noor* (2021)
- Tade Thompson, *Far from the Light of Heaven* (2021)
- Tlotlo Tsamaase, *The Silence of the Wilting Skin* (2020)
- Wole Talabi, ed., *Africanfuturism* (2020)
- Dilman Dila, *A Killing in the Sun* (2014)

Grace L. Dillon's *Walking the Clouds* (2012) describes Indigenous futurism as fantastic modes of fiction by Indigenous writers – including Native American Indians, First Nations, Kanaka Maoli, Maori, Aboriginals – who refuse the often miserabilist burden-of-representation realism expected of such writers while also sidestepping Western sf's generic expectations. Respectful of Indigenous knowledges, lifeways and scientific literacies, Indigenous futurism comes from peoples who have already survived – and are still in the process of surviving – the apocalypse called Western colonialism. Early examples include Martin Cruz Smith's *The Indians Won* (1970), Gerald Vizenor's *Darkness in Saint Louis Bearheart* (1978), William Sanders' *Journey to Fusang* (1988), Misha's *Red Spider White Web* (1990), Sherman Alexie's *Reservation Blues* (1995), Archie Weller's *Land of the Golden Clouds* (1998) and Eden Robinson's *Monkey Beach* (2000). Blake M. Hausman, Stephen Graham Jones, Waubgeshig Rice, Rebecca Roanhorse and Daniel H. Wilson are among the newer writers. YA examples include Ambeline Kwaymullina's *The Interrogation of Ashala Wolf* (2012),* Joseph Bruchac's *Killer of Enemies* (2013)* and Darcie Little Badger's *Elatsoe* (2020). Short films include *File under Miscellaneous* (Barnaby 2010), *Gonawindua* (Cavalli and Suárez 2011), *The Path without End* (LaPensée 2011) and *Hoverboard* (Freeland 2012). Bigger budgets remain elusive, but *American Evil* (Lightning 2008), *The Dead Can't Dance* (Pocowatchit 2010), *Night Raiders* (Goulet 2021), *Prey* (Trachtenberg 2022) and *Slash/Back* (Innuksuk 2022) are among the feature-length efforts, and the TV series *Cleverman* (2016–17) is also noteworthy.

African sf can be traced back at least as far as Egyptian Muhammad Muwaylihi's *A Period of Time* (1898) and the South African settler Joseph J. Doke's *The Secret City* (1913). But the twentieth century saw only a slow accretion of titles, many of them neither published nor immediately recognised as sf. In the new millennium, that changed. There were sf films from Sylvestre Amoussou, Jean-Pierre Bekolo, Neill Blomkamp, Dilman Dila, Nadia El Fani and Wahuri Kahiu, and the first pan-African sf magazine, *omenana* (2014–), was launched. The African Speculative Fiction Society was founded in 2016, which established the Nommo Awards in 2017. And a plethora of original anthologies appeared, including Ivor W. Hartmann's *AfroSF* (2012),* Ayodele Arigbabu's *Lagos 2060* (2013), *Jalada* magazine's *Afrofutures* issue (2015), Nerine Dorman's *Terra Incognita* (2015), Billy Kahora's *Imagine Africa 500* (2015), Jo Thomas and

Margrét Helgadóttir's *African Monsters* (2015), Zelda Knight and Oghenechovwe Donald Ekpeki's *Dominion* (2020) and Sheree Renée Thomas and Ekpeki's *Africa Risen* (2022). By 2021, there was sufficient critical mass for Ekpeki to launch *The Year's Best African Speculative Fiction* (2021) reprint anthology series.

Much of this activity was initially labelled Afrofuturist, but Nnedi Okorafor has instead proposed two other categories, so as to distinguish it from, and keep it from being subsumed into, a mainly African American phenomenon (although all three may at times overlap). Africanfuturism is future-oriented, primarily Black-authored sf, centred in Africa and reaching out into the diaspora, that does not privilege the West. Africanjujuism, which draws on African cosmologies and spiritualities, is its fantasy equivalent.

Naming such trends and traditions helps to make them visible. Perhaps even more importantly, it enables us to see sf anew.

Three

KEY CONCEPTS

→ Afrofuturism

AISHA MATTHEWS

Alongside. Overlapping. Sometimes even within. But different.

Afrofuturism is, first and foremost, a genre of possibility. Coined by Mark Dery in 1993 to describe 'speculative fiction that treats African-American themes and addresses African-American concerns in the context of twentieth century technoculture – and, more generally, African-American signification that appropriates images of technology and a prosthetically enhanced future' (180), Afrofuturism now encapsulates a wide range of artistic productions, modes of thought and philosophical paradigms for the consideration of Black life. It began as a largely African American movement addressing the rift in Black cosmology generated by the Middle Passage and the legacy of American chattel slavery. It has since expanded to include Afrodiasporic productions from the Caribbean and the motherland herself, articulating a shared but varied Black collective consciousness shaped by innumerable Black lifeways.

Afrofuturism explores, elevates and challenges Black life and projects it into the future

In view of the long history of colonial violence – both physical and ontological – and the West's still-active forces of cultural erasure and dehumanisation, it is unsurprising that Afrofuturism's speculative potential is largely consumed with Black futures. What might they look like? What shapes might they take? Which physical, social and cultural adaptations will they require? How will Black cultural production and experience manifest in posthuman worlds of unprecedented possibility?

But far from eliding the traumatic historical roots that recent Afropessimist thinkers have not incorrectly attributed to Black life writ large, Afrofuturism is uniquely situated as a temporal intervention, variously shrinking, inverting, expanding and transcending linear Western traditions to grapple with the remains of the past in our present and future. Afrofuturism often employ alternate histories to reconfigure the meaning of traditional Black forms, such as the antebellum slave narrative, into futuristic formations of neo-slave narratology, simultaneously liberating our ancestral past from its material specificity and transforming it into a lens through which to examine ongoing modes of individual and collective oppression, enslavement and dehumanisation.

Beyond such historical recovery and revisionism, Afrofuturism serves many functions. Some iterations constitute science-fictional interventions into biopolitical and necropolitical examinations of technoculture, surveillance, gender and environmentalism. Others offer a supernatural intervention into the non-Western investment in literal and figurative magic. Still others challenge rationalist binary constructions. And some do all these things at once. But in every case, Afrofuturism explores, elevates and challenges Black life and, most importantly, projects it into the future.

Despite sf's own history of racial erasure, Afrofuturism uses the genre's tools to imagine new modes of being while grappling with the open wounds of historical violence and dehumanisation. At the same time, it insists on Black culture's and Black people's permanence in future landscapes, whether bleak or brimming with utopian potential.

Black people have been living in the aftermath of an alien abduction for the last four hundred years – both alien and alienated from our place of origin and wholeness. Afrofuturism is the story we tell to recover what has been lost, find our bearings within the terrain of what is, and chart the stars of a future yet to be written.

Afrofuturist sf

- Jennifer Marie Brissett, *Elysium* (2014)
- Anthony Joseph, *The African Origins of UFOs* (2006)
- Nalo Hopkinson, *Midnight Robber* (2000)
- Samuel R. Delany, *Stars in My Pockets Like Grains of Sand* (1984)
- Octavia E. Butler, *Wild Seed* (1980)*

Onscreen Afrofuturism

- *Sorry to Bother You* (Riley 2018)
- *Black Panther* (Coogler 2018)
- *Janelle Monáe: Dirty Computer* (Donoho and Lightning 2018)
- *Welcome II the Terrordome* (Onwurah 1995)
- *Sankofa* (Gerima 1993)

AISHA MATTHEWS

Poised between sf and fantasy. Refracting chattel slavery.

Set on a world with a single supercontinent called the Stillness, *The Fifth Season* reimagines racialised structural oppression through the treatment of its posthuman 'orogenes', beings who can manipulate thermal and kinetic energy to affect geological change. Despite their crucial role in enabling life on the Stillness' unstable terrain, orogenes are subjugated, feared and controlled. Every few centuries, violent seismic activity imperils all human life on the planet, leaving only geographically separated survivors held together by the 'stonelore', a hegemonically controlled survivalist history meant to combat the loss of knowledge that comes with every catastrophic Fifth Season.

From the technological horrors revealed at node maintenance stations to orogeny's magical 'strange equation', Jemisin skilfully employs sf and fantasy conventions, melding the rational with the inexplicable to recreate the structural relations undergirding chattel slavery. Just as the antebellum South depended upon the labour of the slaves it also feared, humanity on the Stillness is also fatally dependent on the orogenes.

Marginalised yet powerful, reviled yet essential

Marginalised yet powerful, reviled yet essential, the orogenes' abject position underscores the exclusionary processes by which the privileges and responsibilities of the dominant 'race' are assigned.

The Fifth Season also engages the concept of nonlinear time. Its cyclical narrative of construction and revelation embodies the enduring resonance of what Christina Sharpe calls 'hold time'. Described by Kirsten Dillender as a 'space outside of time' (136), hold time is created by the temporal distortion of the slave ship's hold that, in Sharpe's words, 'repeats and repeats and repeats in and into the present' (90). Despite the recurring geographical and historical breaks that destroy all but the most basic continuity of life on the Stillness, orogeny is like Blackness:

as Dillender argues, it 'marks [certain] characters as infinitely expendable, a status so intransigent that it remains even after Fifth Seasons have eclipsed other forms of knowledge' (138–39). The constancy of structural racial oppression and exclusion demands a closer examination of so-called humanity and its tendencies.

Crucially, *The Fifth Season* evokes numerous parallels with Black historical experiences: knowledge lost through catastrophic epistemological breaks and/or overwritten by hegemonic historical narratives; the introduction of an anthropomorphically conceived violent, paternal god who rules through fear; the constant re-emergence of tribalist thinking; exclusionary community policing; violence against those who are misunderstood; and normative surveillance and control of a 'savage' Other, even though, or perhaps because, they might be able to liberate humankind from its existing systems of oppression.

Afrofuturism engages both optimistic and pessimistic visions of Blackness. It grapples with the past and present violence seemingly endemic to the treatment of Black life while simultaneously envisioning a future full of liberatory possibilities. 'Perhaps you think it wrong that I dwell so much on the horrors, the pain', Jemisin writes, 'but pain is what shapes us, after all. We are creatures born of heat and pressure and grinding, ceaseless movement. To be still is to be . . . not alive' (361). A quintessential Afrofuturist novel, *The Fifth Season* aims to transform the orogenes' pain into fuel for a liberatory future – even if they must tear it all down to do so.

> **Nope (Jordan Peele 2022)**
>
> In the conjoined myths of whiteness and the Wild West, where the frontier transmutes into Hollywood, spectacle erases history. Encountering the Other is fraught with peril, whether chimpanzees, horses, UFOs . . . or white eyes. Do not look up. Do not make eye contact. It can get you killed.

JOY SANCHEZ-TAYLOR

Greys. Xenomorphs. Little green men. An alien is never just an alien.

The figure of the alien has taken many forms and iterations, but at the heart of the alien narrative is the question of what society views as Other. Whether the alien is just a humanoid with a different skin colour or a completely different species, it serves as an allegory for what human beings fear or desire. It is a marker of difference, and as such has stood in for many othered groups over the years.

Because the term 'alien' in the US is often associated with immigration and the idea of 'illegal aliens', the alien encounter in American sf commonly signifies white anxieties about the racial other. Early and pulp sf stories often depicted aliens modelled after 'primitive' cultures (a practice both critiqued and upheld in H.G. Wells' *The War of the Worlds* (1898) and its many adaptations). This pattern is also evident in contemporary alien-invasion movies, such as *Predator* (McTiernan 1987),* *Starship Troopers* (Verhoeven 1997)* and *Ender's Game* (Hood 2013), the latter two based, respectively, on Robert A. Heinlein's 1959 and Orson Scott Card's 1985 novels of the same names. Even films set entirely in an alien culture, such as *Avatar* (Cameron 2009),* reiterate the idea of aliens as primitives in need of a white saviour.

> **The alien encounter commonly signifies white anxieties about the racial other**

While there are contemporary sf novels and films with more diverse characters and casts, the majority of sf that addresses alien encounters or invasions still centres on Eurocentric cultures. Because sf has historically been the product of white, Western creators, sf stories involving aliens often revolve around brave white Westerners in conflict with extraterrestrial cultures which seek to conquer them. But as Noah Berlatsky asks, 'What does it mean that all of these novels and films, from *War of the Worlds* more than 100 years ago to *Star Trek: Into Darkness* in 2013, are powered by colonial inversion, a dream of Western imperial violence inflicted upon Westerners?'

The alien-encounter narrative has always had the potential to comment on the complexities of colonisation. Octavia E. Butler's *Lilith's Brood trilogy* (1987–89) reworks the old trope of aliens interbreeding with humans to explore the cost of survival, and the nature of identity, difference and hybridity, in the face of an overwhelmingly powerful colonial force. In Celu Amberstone's 'Refugees' (2004), the varied reactions of two distinct groups of humans relocated to an alien world by lizard-like Benefactors capture the complex relations between these groups while highlighting the resilience of diasporic and Indigenous peoples. Ted Chiang's 'The Story of Your Life' (1998) depicts an alien race, based on cephalopods, who communicate using a nonlinear language. They are non-combative; they come to Earth to exchange knowledge and then leave without conflict. Chiang's depiction of a nonaggressive alien race critiques Western culture's history of refusing cultural exchange with non-Western and colonised groups. Sf narratives such as these demonstrate how the alien encounter can be used to depict alternative views of cultural interaction.

Alien encounters

- Ruthanna Emrys, *A Half-Built Garden* (2022)
- Cadwell Turnbull, *The Lesson* (2019)
- Ian McDonald, *Chaga* (1995)*
- Eleanor Arnason, *A Woman of the Iron People* (1991)
- Gwyneth Jones, *White Queen* (1991)*

Onscreen alien encounters

- *Attack the Block* (Cornish 2011)
- *Monsters* (Edwards 2010)*
- *Alien* (Scott 1979)*
- *Solaris* (Tarkovsky 1972)
- *Quatermass and the Pit* (1958–59)*

→ Nnedi Okorafor, *Binti* (2015)*

JOY SANCHEZ-TAYLOR

Doing the strangest thing. Loving the alien.

Binti is a key example of how sf authors can utilise the trope of the alien as invading Other while also challenging this depiction through the employment of a radical empathy. Okorafor's themes are closely tied to the categorisation of her writing as Africanfuturism – sf that centres African culture and, in doing so, deliberately refuses to privilege white, Western cultural values. And her depiction of radical empathy is closely aligned with a desire for a more evolved human consciousness – defined by Gloria Anzaldúa as an 'alien consciousness' – that looks beyond surface difference and disputes to highlight interconnectivity between beings.

Okorafor's novella, the first of a trilogy, addresses difference and alienation from its very first sentences. The narrator–protagonist, Binti, states, 'I was going to be a pariah' (10) because she has decided to leave her isolated community in southern Africa to attend Oomza Uni, a mixed-species university on another planet.

Creates a sense of profound alterity, then proceeds to dismantle this difference

While her Himba people use their advanced mathematical knowledge to sustain their community, they do not like outsiders and have nothing to do with other cultures who view them as primitive. Her mother tells her, 'You go to that school and you become its slave' (14). Even before Binti meets actual aliens, she has been alienated from her own people because she desires to engage with others.

While travelling to Oomza Uni, Binti's ship is attacked by the tentacled Meduse, an alien species considered to be inherently violent. In sf and horror, tentacles are often used as a marker of extreme difference between species, but tentacled creatures, such as squid and octopi, are also some of the most intelligent animals on the planet. Occupying this contradiction, Okorafor creates a sense of profound alterity, then proceeds to dismantle this difference as her protagonist learns to communicate with the aliens. Binti compares her braided hair, a marker of her Himba culture, to the Meduse's tentacles. By connecting a Black cultural marker to alienness and also to the mythical Medusa, a misunderstood female figure in Greek mythology, Okorafor begins to consider the implications of cultural ignorance.

In *Binti* and its sequels, Okorafor highlights the cost of survival for colonised peoples, particularly women, partly by deploying the figure – common from historical accounts of real-world colonial encounters – of the Indigenous female cultural mediator. Pocahontas, La Malinche and similar women are often depicted as traitors who willingly helped invading Europeans to colonise their homes. But such accounts fail to acknowledge the sacrifices involved in the work of cultural mediation. Binti must become part Meduse in order to perform such a role. And while her first reaction to this change is one of horror, her ability as a 'master harmonizer' and her understanding of the experience of alienation help her quickly come to terms with her difference. Such radical empathy for the alien Other is central to Okorafor's vision for a more enlightened humanity.

> ### *Arrival* (Denis Villeneuve 2016)
>
> Giant spaceships like elongated mushroom caps. Heptapods whose mottled flesh ripples and swells and whose limbs flex like cephalopod tentacles – when they are not jointed like crustacean legs or rigid like banyan roots. These aliens experience time simultaneously, not serially: learning their semasiographic nonlinear written language will change your mind.

Alternate history

GLYN MORGAN

Possible pasts and alternate presents are all about the world as it now exists.

A semi-autonomous genre of speculative fiction, alternate history shares sf's sense of cognitive estrangement generated by a novum. Unlike sf, the starting point, if not the location of the entire narrative, is the historical past rather than the present or future. With roots in the intellectual exercises of historians, such as Winston Churchill's 'If Lee Had Not Won the Battle of Gettysburg' (1931), and in the specific form of utopianism known as uchronie or uchronia, alternate history also, aptly, has its own genealogy.

It first became enmeshed with sf in the pulp era, with Murray Leinster's 'Sidewise in Time' (1934), and has since attracted occasional excursions by sf writers, such as Philip K. Dick's *The Man in the High Castle* (1962) and Terry Bisson's *Fire on the Mountain* (1988). It has also attracted literary authors, as in Philip Roth's *The Plot against America* (2004) and Bernadine Evaristo's *Blonde Roots* (2009), and popular bestsellers, such as Robert Harris' *Fatherland* (1992) and Stephen Fry's *Making History* (1996). Harry Turtledove, S.M. Stirling, Eric Flint and others have forged successful careers almost entirely within the genre.

Alternate histories feature a point of divergence from our own historical time, sometimes called a point of departure or a Jonbar point: in Sophia McDougall's *Romanitas* trilogy (2005–11), emperor Pertinax avoids being overthrown in AD 193; in Curtis Sittenfeld's *Rodham* (2020), Hilary Rodham turns down Bill Clinton's marriage proposal in 1975. As these examples suggest, most narratives cascade historical differences from a simple change in a prominent individual's life, aligning much of the genre with 'the great man theory of history', rather than a historical materialist or structuralist view based on larger systems. Notable

Narratives cascade historical differences from a simple change

exceptions include Kim Stanley Robinson's *The Years of Rice and Salt* (2002), in which an even more virulent Black Death depopulates mid-fourteenth-century Europe, leading to the global dominance of Chinese, Arabic and Indigenous American cultures.

Karen Hellekson's *The Alternate History* (2001) further subdivides alternate histories into nexus stories (set at the point of divergence), true alternate histories (set after the point of divergence has occurred) and parallel-world stories (multiple timelines existing side by side). There are also secret histories, normally based on conspiracy theories, in which historical narratives as we know them are the fiction and 'true' events happened otherwise: for example, Dan Brown's *The Da Vinci Code* (2003) 'reveals' that Jesus had a child with Mary Magdalene and the church has hidden the truth. And there are paleofutures or alternate futures, such as Arthur C. Clarke's *2001: A Space Odyssey* (1968), where a prominent date once in the future has now passed.

In recent years, parallel worlds and alternate timelines have become not only popular in film and television, as in the Polish thriller *1983* (2018) and alternate space-race series *For All Mankind* (2019–), but also an essential ingredient in elaborating and prolonging shared-universe media behemoths such as the Marvel Cinematic Universe and DC Extended Universe.

Alternate histories

- Brooke Bolander, *The Only Harmless Great Thing* (2018)
- Michael Chabon, *The Yiddish Policemen's Union* (2007)
- Jo Walton, *Farthing* (2006)*
- Sesshu Foster, *Atomik Aztex* (2005)
- Mary Gentle, *Ash* (2000)

Onscreen alternate histories

- *The Man in the High Castle* (2015–19)
- *CSA: The Confederate States of America* (Willmott 2004)
- *2009: Lost Memories* (Lee 2002)
- *G.I. Samurai* (Saitô 1979)
- *It Happened Here* (Brownlow and Mollo 1964)

→ **Nisi Shawl, *Everfair* (2016)***

GLYN MORGAN

What if colonialism – and steampunk – played out differently?

Nisi Shawl's alternate history takes the actions of the Fabian Society as its turning point. In 1895, in our history, this British socialist organisation founded the London School of Economics; in *Everfair*, anti-imperialists within their number successfully lobby for the Society to instead fund the purchase of West African land from the Belgian Crown.

Together, the white Fabians, some Black Christian missionary types and local peoples indigenous to the region found the eponymous new nation. Despite having legally purchased the land from King Leopold II, the fledgling country is harried and harassed by agitators working for the so-called Congo Free State. But thanks to superior knowledge of the land and an influx of new technologies created by engineers from Macau – including dirigibles or 'air-canoes', clockwork artificial limbs and steam-powered bicycles – Everfair is able not only to resist the influence of these colonial forces but ultimately to defeat them in open war.

To resist the influence of colonial forces and to defeat them in open war

Perhaps drawing on contradictions in the language of the American Founding Fathers and the realities of that new nation, which patently did not hold all men to be created equal, and on the experience of many postcolonial nations, *Everfair* details the difficulties involved in holding on to the idea of a nation after its founding. Factionalism and differing visions for the direction Everfair should take, not least which side it should fight on in the First World War, threaten to plunge the country into civil war.

Shawl's novel draws heavily upon the bloody colonial history of the Congo region, specifically acknowledging the importance to her research of Adam Hochschild's *King Leopold's Ghost* (1998). But she also exploits the tone and expected course of nineteenth-century utopian projects, particularly those which claim to resolve problems of race or class, and of resettlement projects that shipped free Black Americans and Black British citizens to found new colonies or cities in lands they had never before visited, such as Liberia and Sierra Leone's Freetown. *Everfair* pierces the naïve utopianism of white Europeans and Christian Americans who assume moral superiority over Indigenous peoples, attempt to impose models of behaviour on them or try to subsume them into the nation-building project in a softer and less lethal but no less arrogant manner than Leopold's extractionist colonialism.

Everfair uses alternate history to expose the history of our own timeline: the brutality of colonial rule in West Africa and the rest of the world's knowledge of and indifference towards it. At the same time, the novel calls into question fundamental assumptions about the genre itself. Shawl's use of technological innovations evokes the steampunk subgenre of alternate history. But by setting the novel almost entirely in West Africa and populating it largely with characters of colour, she not only avoids the Victorian colonial triumphalism that steampunk often falls into but highlights quite how odd, uncomfortable and unforgivably unthinking it can be.

***April and the Extraordinary World* (Christian Desmares and Franck Ekinci 2015)**

What if, on the eve of the Franco-Prussian War, an explosion killed Napoleon III? And what if it also destroyed a lab developing a super-soldier serum, and a pair of Komodo dragon test subjects escaped? What soot-shrouded steampunk twentieth century might unfold? What interspecies conflicts ensue?

SHERRYL VINT

What does it mean to be an animal?
Whether human or non-human?

Animal studies is an interdisciplinary field of enquiry that analyses cultural ideas about human/animal difference. Some scholars work explicitly from an ethical commitment to ending human exploitation of animals, while others illuminate the history of human/animal interactions from philosophical or sociological perspectives without advocating for specific modes of interrelation.

Literary animal studies scholars examine patterns of cultural symbolism anchored in human ideas about animals and often take up questions of voice and narrative point of view, grappling with the philosophical conundrum made famous by Thomas Nagel's 'What Is It Like to Be a Bat?' (1974). Drawing particular attention to the word 'like', he insists that we can never truly know the experience or perspective of another species; we can only imaginatively project it. Consequently, such representations remain deeply anthropocentric.

Literature can imaginatively seek to bridge the gap between human and animal experience, and sf critics consider the genre especially well suited to this task. The difficulty of conveying an animal's experience is similar to the challenge of representing the alien. Fredric Jameson's *Archaeologies of the Future* (2005) suggests that images of aliens often represent a desire for otherness rooted in our own potential to be otherwise; that is, they represent a utopian impulse to change ourselves and our social worlds. By challenging or reframing the human/animal boundary, animal studies does comparable work. It demonstrates how Western understandings of this boundary underpin a culture that has separated humans from nature to devastating ecological effect through extractive capitalism, and has dehumanised people of colour and women by equating

We can never truly know the experience or perspective of another species

them with nature (not culture) and body (not mind). Focusing on animals, acknowledging them as ethical kin rather than objectified resources, helps to contest these histories.

Sf and animal studies scholars share many intellectual concerns. They are interested in imagining how the world might be politically and socially otherwise, and how we might reconceptualise what we mean by 'the human'. They ask how we might engage in meaningful exchange with a non-human, whether animal or alien. And they are strongly influenced by philosophers who critique Western metaphysics through the figure of the animal, such as Jacques Derrida in *The Animal That Therefore I Am* (2006), Giorgio Agamben in *The Open* (2002) and, most importantly in this context, Donna Haraway.

Her 'A Cyborg Manifesto' (1985), a critique of the binaries that structure Western thought to the disadvantage of women, colonised people and nature, galvanised an entire generation of sf scholars. She argues that contemporary developments in biology and computer science thoroughly debunk the presumed binaries between humans/animals, organisms/machines and virtual/material. Only the separation of the sciences from the humanities allows Western thought to continue to operate on such shaky foundations, so she calls for a renewal of our intellectual concepts and more collaboration across the disciplines. In doing so, she draws on sf novels by Octavia E. Butler, Samuel R. Delany, Anne McCaffrey, Vonda McIntyre, Joanna Russ, James Tiptree Jr. and John Varley – evidence of the genre's own interest in bridging the science/culture boundary and of its affinity with animal studies.

Sf about animals

- Laura Jean McKay, *The Animals in That Country* (2020)
- Emma Geen, *The Many Selves of Katherine North* (2016)
- Maja Lunde, *The History of Bees* (2015)
- Karen Joy Fowler, *We Are All Completely Beside Ourselves* (2013)
- Karen Traviss, *City of Pearl* (2004)*

Screen sf about animals

- *The Shape of Water* (del Toro 2017)
- *Splice* (Natali 2009)
- *Phase IV* (Bass 1974)
- *The Day of the Dolphin* (Nichols 1973)
- *Planet of the Apes* (Schaffner 1968)

→ | Adrian Tchaikovsky, *Children of Time* (2015)*

SHERRYL VINT

We are not alone. But maybe we are the aliens.

The series of novels beginning with *Children of Time* is an ideal example of animal studies insights informing sf narrative. It is set in a future in which humanity has left Earth because of extreme anthropogenic environmental damage, which has made living on the planet no longer viable for humans, and political polarisation, which has stymied any chance for amelioration. One of the diverging views that doomed the last Earth-based human generation was the question of human pre-eminence over other species. Tchaikovsky equates commitment to anthropocentrism with the mindset that fuelled the settler colonial and extractive capitalist exploitation of nature to the point that the Earth could no longer sustain human life.

In *Children of Time*, a colonisation experiment on a distant planet attempts to 'uplift' monkeys to greater intelligence, a term adapted from David Brin's *Uplift* series (1980–2009), which similarly projected a future in which humans shared culture with non-human species whose intelligence was augmented through genetic engineering. A comparison is instructive. Brin depicts a cross-species future in which the animals are incorporated into Western human culture without requiring its values to develop, only its technologies – for example, to enable spacecraft to be piloted by dolphins. Tchaikovsky, however, grapples with some of the questions central to animal studies. He extrapolates more radically not only from different forms of embodiment but also from the different capacities and evolutionary histories of the species being genetically engineered. The plan to uplift monkeys goes awry and the recipients of genetic enhancement are spiders in

Non-human animals are more socially and cognitively complex than we might presume

Children of Time, octopi in *Children of Ruin* (2019) and crow-ra-ven-magpie hybrids in *Children of Memory* (2022). Thus, while his uplifted species produce some of the same intellectual and technological history we know from the story of hominid evolution, they also take distinctly different paths, at times precisely because they do not have the social capacities characteristic of hominids.

All three novels engage deeply with the science of ethology to invent ways that non-human species might develop a material culture that could achieve spaceflight. They also recognise that arachnid, mollusc and corvid evolution would have different social as well as technological tendencies. The octopi in particular present a compelling figuration because they are a species whose cognition is not centralised (as in primates) but distributed, and thus their phenomenological experience *and* their cogitation are sharply different from our own.

As characters from these distinct cultures meet and interact with one another, Tchaikovsky showcases how non-human animals are more socially and cognitively complex than we might presume from an anthropocentric point of view. And he models a way that the human species must become otherwise so as to live in more egalitarian ways across difference. His ecological vision of multispecies culture anchors new possibilities for the futures, and resoundingly critiques anthropocentrism as an inadequate ethical basis for just sociality.

> ### *Okja* (Bong Joon-ho 2017)
>
> As Fredric Jameson never said, it's easier to imagine genetically engineered superpigs as an adorable charismatic megafauna companion species than it is to imagine the end of agribusiness mendacity over animal welfare, factory farming and slaughterhouses – or of the cruel climate-damaging reduction of living things to commodities.

→ | Climate fiction

REBECCA MCWILLIAMS OJALA BALLARD,
COL ROCHE AND ELENA WELSH

Climate change is real. But how can we represent it?

Climate change is so vast it boggles imagination and comprehension

'Cli-fi', a play on 'sci-fi', describes fiction and film that extrapolate climate change predictions into realistic near futures. It most often refers to works self-consciously produced and marketed as cli-fi since 2012, when the term – coined by Dan Bloom circa 2007 – entered the popular lexicon via a tweet by Margaret Atwood. Over the next decade, a flurry of articles – typically incorporating 'greatest hits' lists of recent works, featuring a few sf writers along with such literary-critical darlings as Atwood, Ian McEwan, Barbara Kingsolver, Nathaniel Rich and David Mitchell – traced the emerging genre's definition, history and political potential. These accounts sometimes elided more expansive histories of fictional engagements with anthropogenic climate change stretching before and beyond the explosion of cli-fi, most notably Octavia E. Butler's *Parable* novels (1993–98). Some have suggested that climate fiction should include works predating contemporary knowledge of planetary-scale human agency, from J.G. Ballard's *The Drowned World* (1962) all the way back to the *Epic of Gilgamesh*.

Climate change is an overwhelming subject. Timothy Morton calls it a 'hyperobject', something so vast it boggles imagination and comprehension. Paradoxically, climate change still tends to recede into the background of anthropocentric stories, a 'not-here, not-now' nonconcern eclipsed by everyday life. Responding to these challenges, climate fiction often contains formal and stylistic innovations that weave individual stories into more expansive scales, such as shifts between different storylines or perspectives and the incorporation of various forms of media. For example, Jesmyn Ward's *Salvage the Bones* (2011), which follows a Mississippi family before and during Hurricane Katrina, features snippets of television and radio broadcasts that explicitly situate the teenaged narrator's experience in larger climatological and cultural contexts. Richard Powers' *The Overstory* (2018) zooms out even further, following nine main characters and incorporating generation-spanning time lapses that inspire wonder at the grandeur of trees.

Beyond these experiments with scale, climate fiction offers fertile ground for many of sf's major concerns. The works themselves engage ambitious themes: ecomodernist technocratic solutions versus nostalgia for 'pure' nature; visions of dystopia and apocalypse rubbing up against utopian visions of new social possibilities; disruptions of the nature/culture binary, with keen attention to how profoundly the human and more-than-human worlds are interwoven; narratives centred on white masculinism and Western science giving way to increasingly diverse authors and characters and substantive engagements with climate justice. They also open new perspectives onto familiar critical issues – both genre turf wars, as the Anthropocene complicates the borders of speculative and realistic fiction by turning the real world ever more fantastically science-fictional, and perennial debates over the political utility of sf, as cli-fi is (optimistically) posited as a possible 'solution' to climate crisis, capable of transforming readers' beliefs and behaviours. These are powerful and important questions, perhaps best answered by thinking of cli-fi not just as the usual suspects produced under that marketing label in the 2010s, but as a more thematically and historically inclusive category of stories that interrogate human life in relation to climate change.

Climate fiction

- E.J. Swift, *The Coral Bones* (2022)
- Alexis Wright, *The Swan Book* (2016)
- Warren Ellis and Jason Howard, *Trees* (2014–20)
- Franz Schätzing, *The Swarm* (2004)
- Maggie Gee, *The Flood* (2004)

Onscreen climate fiction

- *Utopia* (2013–14)
- *Snowpiercer* (Bong 2013)
- *Take Shelter* (Nichols 2011)
- *The Day after Tomorrow* (Emmerich 2004)
- *The Day the Earth Caught Fire* (Guest 1961)

→

Kim Stanley Robinson, *New York 2140* (2017)

REBECCA MCWILLIAMS OJALA BALLARD,
COL ROCHE AND ELENA WELSH

Finding new ways to live. After the oceans rise.

The sharp divide between über-rich and precariat, the uneven experience of climate apocalypse

Set in the flooded but still-mega city of New York after two historical 'pulses' of sea-level rise, the best-selling *New York 2140* grapples with the multifaceted implications of the climate crisis. Like many climate fiction novels, it uses innovative strategies to tell a compelling story at epic scale. The novel rotates through the narratives of ten characters who all live (or camp) in the same forty-storey building: the building's superintendent; the chair of its housing cooperative; a pair of unemployed financial analysts; a police inspector tasked with solving a series of seemingly unrelated cases; a generally insufferable hedge fund trader who takes a surprising turn towards radical politics; a 'cloud star' who streams daring endangered-animal rescues from her airship; two orphans set on discovering sunken treasure; and an omniscient narrator prone to rambling, exposition-heavy monologues. Each offers an idiosyncratically situated perspective on neoliberal disaster capitalism, the sharp divide between über-rich and precariat, and the uneven experience of climate apocalypse. Yet their storylines inevitably intersect when a superstorm strikes the already-waterlogged city, exacerbating class tensions, prompting a massive rent strike and catalysing activist movements and policy reforms. Ultimately, in focusing on collective action rather than frontier-inflected individual adventure, the novel subverts many familiar tropes of apocalyptic fiction.

Robinson is one of the most renowned sf authors working today, and this defining take on the present is a (if not *the*) paradigmatic example of climate fiction. It is perhaps his best-known work of cli-fi, but planetary-scale human-climate interaction has been a constant theme throughout his career, from his break-out *Three Californias* trilogy (1984–90) through his landmark *Mars* (1992–96) and *Science in the Capital* (2004–7) trilogies to *The Ministry for the Future* (2020). Like *New York 2140*, these novels demonstrate Robinson's meticulous knowledge of climate science and policy and his commitment (informed by graduate study under preeminent Marxist theorist Fredric Jameson) to utopian politics. For Robinson, climate fiction is a space to interrogate possibility as well as disaster, and the political collectives that climate resilience may well require.

Like much cli-fi, then, *New York 2140* sets out to prove that literature can play an important role in the climate crisis, but it is often at its least compelling when it tackles this role self-consciously ('So look', one characters exclaims in the first few pages, 'the problem is capitalism'). At its best, the novel dwells not in oversimplified problems or solutions, but in complexity, and it certainly offers generative material for the many rich questions that preoccupy climate fiction. How does climate change intersect with social (in)justice? What kinds of solutions do different stakeholders propose to the wicked problems of climate change, and what are the possibilities and pitfalls of each? And if, as Robinson ultimately suggests, responding to climate change requires (per Naomi Klein) everything change – social, economic and political as well as technical – how can we generate the imagination and will to enact these transformations?

Nuoc 2030 (Nguyen-Vo Nghiem-Minh 2014)

The year is 2030. Rising seas have inundated the Mekong Delta, capitalism indifferently persists and peasants in stilt houses now fish in the waters directly above and within the borders of the fields they once farmed. A low-key everyday tale about cooking, romance, displacement, murder, biopiracy, corporate espionage, extreme weather and uneven development.

→ Contagion

ANNA MCFARLANE

Borders will fail. Then: extinction or transformation?

The theme of contagion in sf can be traced back to Mary Shelley's *The Last Man* (1826), in which a pandemic wipes out the entire human population, bar one. But it only became a consistent motivating concern during the Cold War, when the US was preoccupied with ideological divisions between Soviet communism and its own individualistic capitalism. For example, *Fantastic Voyage* (Fleischer 1966) – novelised by Isaac Asimov, who also wrote a 1987 sequel – tells the story of a submarine and its crew, shrunk to microbial size, infiltrating the body of a defecting Soviet scientist to remove a blood clot from his brain. As the submarine moves through his bloodstream, defensive white blood cells react aggressively to its incursion. Two decades later, Donna J. Haraway argued that the image of the immune system protecting the body (politic) from invaders underpinned the ideology of Ronald Reagan's proposed 'Star Wars' defence system, which aimed to shoot down any Soviet nuclear missiles when they were still in the air. Drawing on the HIV/AIDS epidemic, she suggested it might be better to think of such a defence as an auto-immune deficiency syndrome – one that would destroy, rather than protect, the patient.

The society under threat from the plague can be even more dangerous than the plague itself

Zombie narratives provide another strand in sf's concern with contagion. In the seminal films of George A. Romero, the idea of contagion is turned inwards to focus on the political situation in the US. In *Night of the Living Dead* (1968),* the protagonist, Ben, played by African American actor Duane Jones, struggles to survive the zombie apocalypse and white supremacism, and its conclusion implies that, for some at least, the society under threat from the plague can be even more dangerous than the plague itself.

Contagion also represents the possibility of transformation. In numerous works, epidemics change the nature of identity and human individuality, producing posthuman beings and consciousness. Greg Bear's *Blood Music* (1985) sees everyone infected with noocytes, self-conscious cells which subsume their human hosts into a single global organism with a distributed consciousness. In M.R. Carey's *The Girl with All the Gifts* (2014),* society collapses when fungal spores turn some people into zombies. But some retain their intelligence, and rather than a return to the pre-pandemic status quo, the future might lie with this fungal-human hybrid.

Sf can also function as a means of running scenarios for real and dangerous developments. During the COVID-19 pandemic, *Contagion* (Soderbergh 2011) found new popularity as interested viewers compared its portrayal of a worldwide zoonotic pandemic to the one in which they found themselves. Some considered it prescient since it mapped the virus's trajectory – similar to COVID-19's hypothesised origin – from bats through a Chinese wet market and into the circuits of global commerce. However, this was because the filmmakers intentionally drew on the expertise of epidemiologists and the World Health Organization to create a probable scenario. Nonetheless, its belated success highlights sf's capacity to create not only powerful warnings but also thought experiments to help us prepare and cope with future shocks.

Contagion sf

- Carola Dibbell, *The Only Ones* (2015)
- Emily St. John Mandel, *Station Eleven* (2014)
- Colson Whitehead, *Zone One* (2011)
- Max Brooks, *World War Z* (2006)
- Sakyo Komatsu, *Virus* (1964)

Onscreen contagion sf

- *Pontypool* (McDonald 2008)
- *I Am Legend* (Lawrence 2007)
- *28 Days Later . . .* (Boyle 2002)*
- *Shivers* (Cronenberg 1975)
- *The Andromeda Strain* (Wise 1971)

ANNA MCFARLANE

We are never being; we are always becoming.

When the zombie apocalypse strikes, Candace Chen is working in an unfulfilling publishing job – and unexpectedly pregnant. Promised a significant bonus if she stays on and maintains the office while management flees, she spends her spare time documenting New York's empty, eerily quiet streets.

Severance draws on George A. Romero's *Dawn of the Dead* (1978), in which a group of survivors hole up from the zombie apocalypse in a shopping mall, only to find that the walking dead are drawn there by 'some kind of instinct. Memory of what they used to do. This was an important place in their lives.' Similarly, the victims of *Severance*'s Shen Fever harmlessly repeat routine actions that meant something to them in life, until they die of malnutrition and exhaustion: a fashion student tries on dresses; a suburban mother sets the table for her family; a retail worker folds shirts. Ma's observations on the role of routines in giving structure to our lives becomes a powerful critique of the way they are fundamentally entwined with capitalist systems. She often lists consumer products – 'Shiseido facial exfoliants, Blue Bottle coffee, Uniqlo cashmere' (11) – to show how capitalism transforms routines into profit-making lifestyles. Skincare regimes require specific products; familiar objects on a desk mark out the integration of the self into the workplace. For Candace's parents, first-generation Chinese immigrants, the formation of routine (attending their local Chinese community church) builds a life for them and, after their deaths, routine is the only thing keeping Candace anchored to her world.

The contagion and the globalised capitalist system that propagated it are indistinguishable, and the novel shows this through the connections between China and the US. For example, Shen Fever has a Chinese origin, as does Candace, and she works as

Those ways of being inattentive that have spread, virus-like, throughout the world

a go-between for American companies commissioning repackaged Bibles and Chinese printers. As more and more people succumb to the disease, trade routes and supply chains break down and Candace finally realises that she has to leave New York. She falls in with a band of survivors, led by Bob, who are heading to a shopping mall to form a community. Ma draws connections between the instigation of routines to control workers and the authoritarian Bob's efforts to take control of this new society. In language reminiscent of a manager reviewing a new employee's probation period, he asks Candace: 'How do you like it here so far, being with us, I mean? Do you think we're the right fit for you?' And like many a worker before her, she thinks, 'He asked this in all seriousness, as if I had any other choice' (32).

Cold War narratives often used contagion as a metaphor for covert invasion by ideological Others opposed to capitalist liberal democracy. In contrast, *Severance* makes the reader conscious of the grooves into which we too easily fall – those ways of being inattentive that have spread, virus-like, throughout the world, everywhere fostering mindless reproduction of the capitalist status quo.

In the Earth (Ben Wheatley 2021)

After the virus's third wave, prophylaxes are in effect: lockdown, quarantine, isolation, testing, antivirals, disinfectants, masks, social distancing. But we are embedded in the world and it in us, and fungi are everywhere. Contagion is just another word for totality, for the dirty weird utopia of loved-up, evanescent, terrifying interconnectedness.

ANNA MCFARLANE

Future's so blighted I gotta wear mirrorshades.

Taking its name from the title of a 1982 Bruce Bethke story, the cyberpunk movement found its manifesto in Bruce Sterling's preface to *Mirrorshades: The Cyberpunk Anthology* (1986). Sterling described a group of writers – centrally, Pat Cadigan, William Gibson, Rudy Rucker, Lewis Shiner and John Shirley – as members of an sf avant-garde bringing new blood and new ideas into the genre. They were fascinated with the ways technology could be remixed and reimagined via a do-it-yourself punk aesthetic. Body modification, computers, virtual reality and experimental drug use were among their common themes.

Although Sterling's anthology brought together ten authors and a dozen stories, one writer, and arguably one text, really set the agenda for cyberpunk and its legacy. William Gibson's *Neuromancer* (1984)* combined the plot of a heist movie with the aesthetics of a noir detective story and added a visionary, poetic description of the nonspace behind the computer screen, for which he coined the term 'cyberspace'. This vision of a new digital frontier, peopled by outlaw hackers and in danger of monopolisation by corporations and other vested interests, immediately offered a means of imagining the future of the (as yet) infant internet – and a playground for other writers who were quick to take up Gibson's ideas. Neal Stephenson's *Snow Crash* (1992), for example, imagines cyberspace as the 'Metaverse', where avatars roam and communicate with one another. It in turn inspired the proto-social media online space Second Life, and re-emerged in 2021 as Mark Zuckerberg laid out his plans for Facebook to invest in creating a Metaverse that would combine virtual reality with the physical world in increasingly integrated ways. In cinema, the light cycles of *TRON* (Lisberger 1982)* drew paths of neon in the blackness of cyberspace, and *Blade Runner* (Scott

Body modification, computers, virtual reality and experimental drug use

1984)* gave the definitive aesthetic of the noirish, neon futuristic cityscape, defined by its grime and advertising saturation.

Since the 1980s, cyberpunk has become a set of cultural motifs and practices that can be put to work in understanding techno-saturated societies, its tropes and aesthetics appearing in many different contexts. For example, Janelle Monáe portrays herself as the android Cindi Mayweather on her albums and in their accompanying 'emotion pictures', using this non-human persona to interrogate the factors that shape identity, particularly race, gender and sexuality. Cyberpunk has also contributed to cyberactivism. There was early cross-pollination between cyberpunk authors and the Electronic Frontier Foundation, an organisation that set out to ensure that the new frontier of the internet would be open to everyone. Sterling's non-fiction *The Hacker Crackdown* (1992) traces this history, showing how the early hackers posed a problem for capitalism's drive to consume the open spaces of the internet commons. Jaron Lanier and Cory Doctorow, notable figures in these fights, have long engaged with cyberpunk, the former influencing the look of virtual technologies in *Strange Days* (Bigelow 1995) and *Minority Report* (Spielberg 2002), the latter writing *Down and Out in the Magic Kingdom* (2004) and *Little Brother* (2008).*

Cyberpunk

- Chen Qiufan, *Waste Tide* (2013)
- G. Willow Wilson, *Alif the Unseen* (2012)
- Lauren Beukes, *Moxyland* (2008)
- Melissa Scott, *Trouble and Her Friends* (1994)
- Pat Cadigan, *Fools* (1992)

Onscreen cyberpunk

- *Avalon* (Oshii 2001)*
- *The Matrix* (Wachowskis 1999)*
- *eXistenZ* (Cronenberg 1999)
- *New Rose Hotel* (Ferrara 1998)
- *Akira* (Ōtomo 1988)

→ | Larissa Lai, *The Tiger Flu* (2018)

ANNA MCFARLANE

Living in the chinks of the corporate world machine.

In Larissa Lai's dystopian future, the eponymous zoonotic virus has decimated the male population. There is no cure, and most infected men die; others live in squatter communities, their illness visible in the weeping sores on their faces. While dying men roam the crumbling metropolis of Saltwater City, young women at the Cordova School for Dancing Girls are taught the choreography of thievery and disguise. Beyond the city, in the fourth quarantine zone, the Grist Village houses a troupe of women who fled the city generations before and carry on their traditions of genetic modification, cloning and organ transplantation. Kirilow Groundsel is a 'groom', partnered with a 'starfish' whose limbs and organs regrow if they are damaged – or harvested for transplant. In the satellites Chang and Eng, some people are being uploaded, leaving their bodies behind in an effort to find a better life, while those on the ground are left to struggle for resources, to feed off leftover tinned food from the time before, to scrounge what energy they can from solar panels in this time after oil.

Lai's novel shows how cyberpunk themes are being remixed in the encounter with the climate crisis. Technologies reminiscent of 1980s cyberpunk's body modification and virtual reality themes remain. Characters can plug 'scales' into their brains, which give them different memories and skills, as in Williams Gibson's 'Johnny Mnemonic' (1981) and *Neuromancer* (1984).* They can also be uploaded into a virtual environment, and flesh-and-blood characters can enter the virtual reality to visit them, recalling earlier cyberpunk's transhumanist fantasy of separating the mind from the body and leaving the meat behind. However, technology signifies differently in *The Tiger Flu*, which is steeped in awareness of Asian cultures, Indigenous practices and energy concerns.

Young women are taught the choreography of thievery and disguise

There is a division at the heart of the story world. Saltwater City, inhabited by 'Salties' and controlled by the corporation HöST, is the home of technology. But in the Grist Village, Kirilow considers processed medicine from the time before, such as ibuprofen pills or morphine injections, to be 'poison'. 'Gristies' practice their own medicine, using common plants as healing herbs, which Lai frames as being analogous to the traditions of Indigenous people.

However, any simple opposition between modernity and tradition is undone by the fact that Gristie culture is based on genetic manipulation, including cloning, which we would normally understand as futuristic. This suggests that Indigenous knowledge should be considered a different form of technology, parallel to Western science, rather than a practice located in a pre-technological past. At the same time, though, the Gristie women are dead set against the idea of uploading consciousness and abandoning the body. The technological dream of reducing the mind to pure data – dreamed by *Neuromancer*'s console-cowboy Case and numerous others – is not only adapted but also critiqued in Lai's dense, surreal, evocative vision of a climate-crisis cyberpunk future.

Possessor **(Brandon Cronenberg 2020)**

When you can upload your consciousness into other people's brains to control their bodies, it should be a lot easier to be a wife, mother and corporate assassin. Even with the cognitive, affective and corporeal dissonance. But everything bleeds: targets, hosts, loved ones, memories, identities – reality itself.

DAVID HARTLEY

Different bodies. Different capacities. Different possibilities.

Disability theory is never too far away from science-fictional thinking. Reflections on the lives of disabled people by disabled people, whether in the oppressive past or the vulnerable present, soon turned to questions of what a disabled future should look like. Too often, the non-disabled assume the future of a disabled individual is, at best, stalled, endlessly waiting within a perpetual present moment, anticipating the development of a miracle cure or a perfected prosthetic. Disability theory and activism want to reclaim unimagined futures.

Shifting the emphasis from a purely medical understanding to a focus on accessibility and social stigma reconfigures disability: no longer a hopeless tragedy but a different embodiment, rich with potential, pleasures and insights. Cripping – that is, upsetting normality to defiantly demonstrate alternative possibilities – repositions disability, transforming it into a political force that can speak back to hegemonies of normalcy. Sf's alien embodiments, posthuman interfaces and sensory excesses offer a bountiful imaginary with which to generate crip destabilisations.

Upsetting normality to defiantly demonstrate alternative possibilities

Historically, sf has treated disability in one of two reductive ways: as a visual marker of loss and chaos in dystopian wastelands, or as something to be swiftly erased by technological advances. In superhero and supervillain origin stories, the trauma of bodily or cognitive affliction is typically a catalyst for the pursuit of their ideological destinies. In such 'narrative prosthesis', disability performs a metaphoric role for the benefit of non-disabled protagonists or produces a compensatory 'supercrip' status that most real disabled people would struggle to achieve (Mitchell and Snyder 9).

However, sf's tendency to foreground bodily variation opens up narrative spaces in which to reimagine the agency of disabilities. The stories collected in Kathryn Allan and Djibril Al-Ayad's *Accessing the Future* (2015) place disabled bodies in the weightlessness of space travel, augment them with mechs, adorn them with wearable tech that renders invisible disabilities visible. There is still suffering and pain – such issues of course remain important to disabled experience – but there is also a collective yearning for interdependence, where collaboration, care and support wins the day.

Sf often recognises that to be disabled is to find advantage in disadvantage. In John Scalzi's *Lock In* (2014), a pandemic permanently paralyses a proportion of sufferers, but before a cure can be discovered, an innovation in virtual reality provides the disabled with a community they then become reluctant to lose. The chronically ill 'sky surgeon' of Jacqueline Koyanagi's *Ascension* (2013) uses her relationship with constant pain to develop the resolute stubbornness that enables her to push harder and further than those who might otherwise write her off.

As we collectively face a catastrophic future of environmental breakdown, mass migration and the continual spectres of pandemic and conflict, the ableist assumption of 'technology as cure' (Allan 9) no longer applies. Perhaps it never did. Instead, cripped sf offers vital parables of cooperation over eradication, and rejects the demands of impossible norms to embrace the possibilities of variation.

Disability in sf

- ◘ Nalo Hopkinson, *Sister Mine* (2013)
- ◘ Liz Jensen, *The Rapture* (2009)
- ◘ Kazuo Ishiguro, *Never Let Me Go* (2005)
- ◘ Larissa Lai, *Salt Fish Girl* (2002)
- ◘ Lois McMaster Bujold, *Falling Free* (1988)*

Disability in screen sf

- ◘ *Source Code* (Jones 2011)
- ◘ *Transfer* (Lukacevic 2010)
- ◘ *Blindness* (Mereilles 2008)
- ◘ *Gattaca* (Niccol 1997)
- ◘ *The Incredible Shrinking Man* (Arnold 1957)

→ | Mira Grant, *Into the Drowning Deep* (2017)

DAVID HARTLEY

Mermaids are real. And so is cripped sf.

'The problem with trying to define nature is that nature is bigger than we are, and nature doesn't care whether we know how to define it' (208). So remarks Dr Jillian Toth, the resolute 'sirenologist', when her theory that mermaids really exist is proved beyond doubt. She is on board *The Melusine*, a luxury research ship funded by an entertainment corporation with a vested interest in the sirens who lurk in the depths of the Mariana Trench. Joining Toth are her ex-husband, Theo Blackwell, who suffers with chronic pain; the Wilson twins, Heather and Holly, who are congenitally deaf; and Olivia, an autistic reporter. By pitting this ensemble of disabled protagonists against killer mermaids, Grant demonstrates that human nature is bigger and more complex than the perceived ideal of non-disabled existence.

She does not sanitise or romanticise the experience of disability, and she does give the possibilities afforded by technology their due. Blackwell's chronic pain was caused by a maritime accident, and 'advances in nerve regeneration' (69) have prevented paralysis, while autonomous cars enable him to stay active and mobile. As the sinister corporate representative luring naïve scientists to their doom, he appears to be a classic disabled villain, rendered monstrous by his condition. But through exposure to his experience of pain, we come to understand his voyage as one of damage limitation; the killer mermaids will be encountered, so it is best done, he contends, with plentiful funding and expertise.

Bigger and more complex than the perceived ideal of non-disabled existence

While flawed in practice, this is nevertheless an insight derived from the complex embodiment of disability. The 'curative imaginary' (Kafer 27–28) writes off disabled futures, but the disabled themselves bring divergent knowledge and experience to unexplored realms, and they are braced and resilient. Blackwell describes hiring the Wilson twins as 'winning the lottery' (113). In addition to their credentials (Heather is a submersible operator, Holly a marine biologist), they use a non-verbal language, which might prove useful in opening up cross-species communication with a captured mermaid and, in turn, may lead to cooperative understanding rather than mutual annihilation.

Here deafness is a boon, not a flaw, and disability is an embodied advantage rather than a narrative prosthetic for the non-disabled. Heather takes great pride in the prospect of being the first diver to reach the bottom of the Mariana Trench and thus an inspiration 'for every deaf girl with a dream who came after her' (148). As she descends, with the mermaids watching, she feels 'perfectly at home' in the 'soundless depths' (146), finding kinship with the blind fish of the deep who get by just fine without sight.

By emphasising the possibilities of disability and never questioning the presence of its disabled characters, *Into the Drowning Deep* crips the survivalist sf thriller. Fittingly for a narrative which must lure us into believing in mermaids, the 'natural' and 'normal' are questioned and subverted. And a disabled reader can see themselves not written out but part of the future.

A Quiet Place* (John Krasinski 2018)

They hunt by sound. If you're deaf, you can't hear them coming or the noises that might betray you. But apocalypse rewrites sociocultural norms. Now the hearing mutely inhabit the silence. And everyone signs because speaking aloud is a kind of disability – and it will get you killed.

→ Dystopia

SARAH LOHMANN

The worst of all possible worlds? The actually-existing one.

Dystopian fiction is concerned with how the world might be otherwise. Like utopian fiction, it extrapolates from and thus critiques existing social norms and tendencies. However, while utopias imagine societies in a better state, a dystopia presents 'a non-existent society described in considerable detail and normally located in time and space that the author intended a contemporaneous reader to view as considerably worse than the society in which that reader lived' (Sargent 9).

The term 'dystopia' was first employed in an 1868 parliamentary speech by John Stuart Mill, but dystopia's roots run deeper. Quasi-dystopian works, such as Hannah More's *The History of Mr Fantom* (1787) and Mary Shelley's *Frankenstein* (1818), satirised the idealisation of reason around the French revolution – although they might be better described as 'anti-utopias' that critique specific utopias or utopianism per se and lack dystopia's traces of hope for something better.

Dystopian social dreaming came more into its own in the late nineteenth century: in novels such as H.G. Wells' *The Time Machine* (1895) and *The Island of Doctor Moreau* (1896), which extrapolate from the Industrial Revolution's rapid scientific progress and urbanisation, but retain the hope that intelligent social organisation might avert such dire outcomes. However, the novels most associated with dystopia – Yevgeny Zamyatin's *We* (1924), Aldous Huxley's *Brave New World* (1932), George Orwell's *Nineteen Eighty-Four* (1949) – emerged at a time so bleak as to seem hopeless. Prompted by the horrors of world war, these thought experiments envisioned totalitarian societies that use scientific and technological advances to control people, language, logic and memory. *Brave New World*'s caste system is produced through eugenic science, and a combination of drugs,

More dissonant than dissident, he nonetheless represents hope

sex and spectacular media keeps everyone in their place; *We* and *Nineteen Eighty-Four* focus more on brutal state power and the loss of identity. Orwell, an anti-Stalinist concerned with the corrupting effect of power worship, depicts various tools of subjugation, including the cult of personality, surveillance, violent scapegoating rituals, rewriting history and curtailing the means of expression, but is more interested in asking whether one would allow oneself to be controlled – or to become one of the controllers. His protagonist, like those of Zamyatin and Huxley, does not quite fit in; more dissonant than dissident, he nonetheless represents hope.

Classical dystopias thus stand apart from the pessimism and techno-scepticism of other pre-1970s sf. But they share battle-hardened optimism with such 'critical dystopias' as Marge Piercy's *He, She and It* (1991) and Octavia Butler's *Parable of the Sower* (1993), which 'negotiate the necessary pessimism of the generic dystopia with an open, militant utopian stance that not only breaks through the hegemonic enclosure of the text's alternative world but also reflexively refuses the anti-utopian temptation that lingers in every dystopian account' (Baccolini and Moylan 7).

Dystopias thus maintain the bright light of utopia in their negative image. And it is their science-fictionality that enables them to do so, because the process of extrapolation builds from the conjuncture at which society sets the gears for disaster – or chooses a better world.

Dystopias

- Samit Basu, *The City Inside* (2020)
- Jennie Melamed, *Gather the Daughters* (2017)
- Mohamed Rabie, *Otared* (2014)
- Sabrina Vourvoulias, *Ink* (2012)
- Nnedi Okorafor, *Who Fears Death* (2010)*

Screen dystopias

- *The Hunger Games* (Ross 2012)*
- *Children of Men* (Cuarón 2006)
- *THX 1138* (Lucas 1971)
- *Alphaville* (Godard 1965)
- *Metropolis* (Lang 1927)

SARAH LOHMANN

It's closer than you might think. Much closer.

Red Clocks is a feminist dystopia about reproductive justice and the politics of women's bodies. In a near-future US, the 'Personhood Amendment' has given constitutional rights to fertilised eggs, making abortion illegal and outlawing IVF (since embryos cannot give consent); a ban on single-parent adoption is also imminent. These new laws are the only discernible changes in a world otherwise and increasingly much like our own. As real-world changes to abortion laws turn the cause of women's bodily autonomy back half a century, one can only echo the lament: 'how many horrors are legitimated in public daylight, against the will of most of the people' (173).

Sharing key concerns with Margaret Atwood's dystopian *The Handmaid's Tale* (1985), *Red Clocks* also alludes to Joanna Russ' utopian *The Female Man* (1975) by following four women at odds with patriarchal expectation. Here, however, they are distinct individuals, initially referred to by their roles in one another's stories. Ro, 'the biographer' of nineteenth-century polar explorer Eivør Mínervudottír, struggles to get pregnant on her own. Mattie, 'the daughter', is fifteen, pregnant and unable to get an abortion. Susan, 'the wife', loves her two children but leads an unfulfilling domestic life. Gin, 'the mender', identifies as a forest witch and provides reproductive healthcare to women with nowhere else to turn. They are suffocating under the weight of unjust legislation, surrounded by a roaring sea of uncaring men in their small coastal town. And just as Mínervudottír was trapped in pack ice, so their life plans are stifled and their 'red clocks' (wombs) in danger of being grasped by cold, calculating misogyny. Ro must adopt before it is illegal, Mattie must find a way to abort her pregnancy, Susan must leave her husband and Gin must face accusations of medical malpractice. Their plights connect

The weight of unjust legislation, a roaring sea of uncaring men

them to women across history – ordinary women, scholars like Mínervudottír who had to publish under another's name and the healers and teachers executed as witches. As Gin notes, she is 'one of many' and at least 'they aren't allowed to burn her' (255).

At first, the four women, 'too tired to be furious' (252), are set against each other through conditioned jealousy, but they come to realise they can only liberate themselves if they liberate one another. They find strength in community with their long-suffering foremothers, including Gin and Mattie's witch ancestor, who lives on in Gin's potions, and Mínervudottír, who, thanks to Ro's biography, lives on in 'other brains' (347). Emerging from their struggles not as individuals divided by the patriarchy but as a network of strong women who look out for each other, the four finally perceive one another clearly – not through a patriarchal lens, but as sisters – and are thus able to 'see what is [and] what is possible' (349). By maintaining this utopian impulse, *Red Clocks* joins 'the struggle to articulate the emergence of the female subject in a context in which female agency continues to experience profound limitations' (Wolmark 91).

Mad Max: Fury Road (George Miller 2015)

In the ruins of it all, the present persists. On the one hand, resource-hoarding women-enslaving brutal toxic hierarchical pallid thanatropic petrocultural patriarchy. On the other, multigenerational seed-preserving water-sharing women of colour and pallor and their allies. It's time to draw a line in the sand.

→ Gender

KATIE STONE

If gender is an ideological construct, why not build differently?

A common complaint among critics interested in gender is that sf has not lived up to its subversive potential. All too often, readers find themselves in a far-flung galaxy or distant future in which gender roles remain entirely familiar. Feminists find themselves with questions. Who is caring for these spacefarers' children? How might advances in robotics change our understanding of what makes a body desirable? Why do all these lady aliens want to kiss Captain Kirk?

The complaint of 1970s feminist sf writers – that mainstream sf is hostile to women, with female characters either absent or merely props in male-dominated dramas – still resonates.

Why do all these lady aliens want to kiss Captain Kirk?

For example, the long-awaited *Blade Runner 2049* (Villeneuve 2017) has even more scenes of gendered violence against female replicants than *Blade Runner* (Scott 1982), joining sf productions such as *Ex Machina* (Garland 2014) and *Westworld* (2016–) in the literal objectification of women. Contemporary sf's misogyny also has a real-world component, demonstrated by the 2014 formation of the 'Sad Puppies' Hugo Award voting bloc, which tried to prevent women winning because they do not write 'real' sf. For a woman and/or queer person to engage in sf fandom is to risk a torrent of abuse.

Much of this recent misogyny can, however, be attributed to the growing presence of queer and feminist voices. In 2021, all five finalists for the Best Novel Hugo were women. The success of authors such as N.K. Jemisin, Nnedi Okorafor, Charlie Jane Anders and Aliette de Bodard shows that the 1970s feminist sf boom was not a blip in an otherwise conservative history and that the genre provides an ideal arena for challenging supposedly natural gender roles. When one can augment oneself with technological prostheses, like Tan-Tan in Nalo Hopkinson's *Midnight Robber* (2000), or fuse with artificial intelligences, like characters in Benjanun Sriduangkaew's *And Shall Machines Surrender* (2019), or transform one's own body at will, like the protagonist of Andrea Lawlor's *Paul Takes the Form of a Mortal Girl* (2017), why would one accept the body they were born with as a definitive guide to their character?

These exciting experiments with gender do not shy away from the genre's fascination with technology. Contemporary sf authors tend to reject the misogynist, essentialist notion that women are innately drawn to nature. In this, they follow Donna Haraway, who argues that sf's hybrid human/animal/machine beings offer more to feminism than the second wave's Earth mothers. By creating ostentatiously unnatural bodies, Haraway contends, sf prompts readers to consider our own unnaturalness: how our bodies are affected by the technologies with which we interact and the chemicals we consume, as well as by our complicated relationships to one another. While the cyborg is not always a figure of liberation – for every pleasurable, queer remaking of the body, there is the threat of forcible transformation into a Stepford Wife – its ubiquity does demonstrate the central relevance of gender to sf.

While the puppies sadly yap about what they think is theirs, Haraway's cyborgs flourish.

Sf about gender

- Anne Charnock, *Dreams before the Start of Time* (2017)
- Monica Byrne, *The Girl in the Road* (2014)
- Becky Chambers, *The Long Way to a Small, Angry Planet* (2014)*
- Johanna Sinisalo, *The Core of the Sun* (2013)
- Gwyneth Jones, *Life* (2002)

Screen sf about gender

- *Teknolust* (Hershman-Leeson 2002)
- *Orlando* (Potter 1992)
- *Born in Flames* (Borden 1983)
- *The Stepford Wives* (Forbes 1975)
- *The End of August at the Hotel Ozone* (Schmidt 1967)

KATIE STONE

Spaceships. Space battles. Gestational labour. Reproductive justice.

The Stars Are Legion is a space opera, a grand and bloody tale of adventure and revenge. Centred on the Legion, a collection of world-ships ruled over by despotic warlords, it follows the conflict between Lords Katazyrna and Bhavaja, who vie for the power to create new worlds. They send armies equipped with terrifying chemical weapons hurtling through space against one another, consuming the material of their worlds in increasingly desperate power grabs that threaten the future of the Legion and thus of life as they know it.

It is also a novel entirely about women: from the Lords of the Legion to those who inhabit the bowels of the world-ships, all the characters are female. It thus reshapes hard sf from within. The 'brutal women' to whom the book is dedicated have carved out a space in the genre where traditional binaries between masculinity and femininity, between hard and soft science, no longer hold. This is a story about warrior women who would find laughable the idea that being female means being gentle, caring and ill-suited for space battles.

For them, to be human is to be female

The Legion is the latest in a long history of all-female societies in sf, from the land of *Mizora* (1880–81), which Mary E. Bradley Lane imagined existing within the hollow Earth, to the plague-ridden planet Jeep, depicted in Nicola Griffith's *Ammonite* (1992). However, while the women in previous separatist utopias escaped from, defeated or survived patriarchal oppression, Hurley's women have never known men. For them, to be human is to be female, and thus they have no conception of gendered oppression. In *The Stars Are Legion*, people cannot be neatly divided into two supposedly exclusive categories. It is neither a utopia built on the perceived natural superiority of one half of the human race, nor a dystopia designed to prove that women are somehow 'just as bad' as men. Rather, in creating a complex world without binary gender, Hurley shows that the absence of misogyny would not instantaneously alleviate all other modes of oppression. In this novel, a person's suitability for creating a utopia is not tied to an accident of birth but to their commitment to freedom.

That is not to say that Hurley is not interested in birth. Indeed, there are many pregnancies in the novel, with the women of the Legion gestating not only children but any spare part their world-ship requires. The supposedly natural bonds between mothers and children are made strange as women cradle inanimate objects and swap wombs for better parts. Here, the central tenet of Marxist feminism – that reproductive labour is the work that sustains the global economy – is literalised. Hurley demonstrates that the politics of reproductive justice are intimately tied to those of world governance. In *The Stars Are Legion*, the bloody violence of gestational labour cannot be dismissed as a niche 'women's issue' but is instead central to the crafting of new, science-fictional worlds.

> **Advantageous (Jennifer Phang 2015)**
>
> It's the neoconservative mid-twenty-first century, hypercapitalism is even more hyper, 'inner beauty' still doesn't cut it and suddenly you're too old and too Asian to be the face of the product and your one shot at making a better future for your daughter is to somehow get a younger, whiter body...

HUGH C. O'CONNELL

The production of uniformity.
The production of difference.

Because of globalisation's relationship to cultural and economic neo-imperialism, it can be difficult to separate from postcolonialism. Indeed, the two can often be read and thought of in relation to one another: just as the legacies of imperialism and settler colonialism inform the development of globalisation, so globalisation opens the door to economic, political and cultural neo-imperialism. One way to distinguish between them, however, is to focus on the *neo-* of neo-imperialism. Doing so helps to reveal the political, cultural and economic contradictions of uneven development that result in the seemingly contradictory processes of standardisation and differentiation undergirding globalisation.

In this light, globalisation describes a number of multivalent, and at times contradictory, cultural, political and economic policies arising out of the post-imperial and post–Cold War period. In terms of standardisation, globalisation signals the shrinking of the world: temporally, through the digital immediacy of the internet and computerisation; economically, through global finance and geographically dispersed commodity and production chains and distribution systems; politically, through the enforcement of neoliberal policies by the World Bank, the International Monetary Fund, the World Trade Organization and other supranational entities; and culturally, through the commodification and dissemination of cultural products, from Disney's Marvel films to K-pop. Together, these interrelated shrinkings lead to globalisation's dominant spatial metaphor – the global village – that highlights the sense of a singular, post-national world loosely circumscribed and held together by these forces.

Increases immiseration for many while sustaining plenty for a select few

Sf has long imagined various utopian/dystopian world-states as the rational endpoint of global modernisation, including the post-national futures of H.G. Wells' *A Modern Utopia* (1905) and

Star Trek's (1966–69) Federation. In these examples, globalisation tends to denote a sense of standardisation, centralisation and uniformity, perhaps best exemplified by the franchise model of capitalism, which means you can order an identical grande mocha latte seemingly anywhere in the world.

But a lot of contemporary sf focuses on the other half of globalisation's dialectic: differentiation. Despite uniting the world through the extension of the capitalist market, global modernisation proceeds through uneven development and the production of difference. Globalisation thus relegates certain populations and areas to underdeveloped sweatshops while elevating others to overdeveloped financial hubs, thereby perpetuating a global system that increases immiseration for many while sustaining plenty for a select few. While older sf models of the world-state were invoked as a rational solution to alleviate such economic, social and political discrepancies, more recent sf like Chen Qiufan's *Waste Tide* (2013) and Nnedi Okorafor's *Lagoon* (2014) focuses on the ways that the actually existing structures of late capitalist globalisation exacerbate such unevenness.

In mapping uneven development while at the same time desiring to decentre the 'uniform' capitalist futures dictated by the economic powers of the global north, globalisation in sf rebounds with postcolonial sf, whether as dystopian critiques or as utopian projections of alternative political possibilities.

Sf about globalisation

- ⬚ Geoff Ryman, *Air* (2005)
- ⬚ David Mitchell, *Cloud Atlas* (2004)
- ⬚ Manjula Padmanabhan, *Harvest* (1998)
- ⬚ Karen Tei Yamashita, *Tropic of Orange* (1997)
- ⬚ Bruce Sterling, *Islands in the Net* (1988)

Screen sf about globalisation

- ⬚ *Sense8* (2015–18)
- ⬚ *District 9* (Blomkamp 2009)
- ⬚ *Code 46* (Winterbottom 2003)
- ⬚ *Demonlover* (Assayas 2002)
- ⬚ *Until the End of the World*, director's cut (Wenders 1991)

HUGH C. O'CONNELL

What if big data could actually make a better world?

Literary critics often present 1980s cyberpunk as the paramount cultural expression of late-capitalist globalisation. Slickly self-branded and marketised, cyberpunk grittily extrapolated the asocial market-oriented neoliberalism promoted by Reagan and Thatcher. It depicted hustle-or-perish antiheroes in borderless mega-sprawls of corporate enclaves and urban dilapidation. It imagined the immaterial circulation of information as value, the replacement of civil governance by corporate management and the commodification of all aspects of culture and life. Forty-plus years later, its narrative protocols are still being refined and employed in post-cyberpunk works like *Infomocracy*.

Rather than merely emulating or rebooting classical cyberpunk, Older updates its best features, employing taut thriller pacing and packing in big ideas, for a world in which globalisation and neoliberalism are no longer newly emerging ideologies but the dominant aspects of local and supranational governance. Forgoing the sexist baggage and disaffected cynicism that often undermined even the best of classical cyberpunk, *Infomocracy*

The centrality, currency and circulation of information and computing

focuses on the centrality, currency and circulation of information and computing, and their impact on globalisation and governance. It examines problems of political polarisation, the online proliferation of disinformation and the anti-democratic centralisation of ubiquitous computing and surveillance by monopoly corporate giants like Google, Apple and Meta, and it recasts these real-world problems as opportunities to imagine solutions to our decreasing autonomy and democracy.

Channelling globalisation's contradictory tendencies towards standardisation and differentiation into its world-building, *Infomocracy* imagines the creation of a totally centralised global informational bureaucracy, called Information, that controls all data circulation (monitoring for disinformation, illegal activity and so on). This standardisation is counterposed by a new post-national world-system of micro-democracy, whereby most nation-states have been replaced by cantons of no more than 100,000 citizens. Elections take place every ten years, and each canton's citizens vote for one party from a vast multitude covering the full gamut of the political positions, with the party that wins the most cantons designated as the supermajority.

Infomocracy follows the intrigue surrounding a crisis in Information and its political fallout as various parties vie for the supermajority. Older draws on her significant academic and professional experience in humanitarian aid, disaster relief and governance throughout the novel and its sequels, *Null States* (2017) and *State Tectonics* (2018), to portray the richly detailed inner workings of the political organisations and systems that dominate her imagined future. Thus, the trilogy's biggest – and most welcome – departure from classical cyberpunk is the way it flips the emphasis from corporate control and commodification to the practicalities of governance, elections and socially benefiting bureaucracies. By replacing cyberpunk's animating cynicism and anti-human values with a utopian drive to reimagine how these tools can be used for humanity's social benefit, Older presents a starkly different yet utterly believable alternative to our current experience of globalisation.

> ### *Jupiter's Moon* (Kornél Mundruczó 2017)
>
> Borders maintain colonial power and deny humanity to others. But the spice must flow, no matter how violent and grubby the world it makes. Corporate logos, French fries and ethnonationalism are everywhere. When Syrian refugees are attacked, something new is born: he's no angel, but you'll believe a man can fly.

→ | Hard sf

SHERRYL VINT

Abide by the rules. Except when you don't.

'Hard sf' was coined in 1957 by sf author P. Schuyler Miller in his *Astounding* book review column. Often understood as fiction that extrapolates from science, hard sf more typically develops from a deep connection to engineering. It focuses on developments in spaceship, computer, energy, weapon and other technologies, and is invested in detailed descriptions of how new inventions or insights create something novel in the narrative world. It privileges pure sciences, such as physics and mathematics, but has more recently welcomed chemistry and biology, although only as these disciplines have become more engineering oriented, as in genetics and synthetic biology.

The term emerged out of an ongoing discussion between writers, editors, critics and fans about the key characteristics that identify a work as sf. Some, such as Hugo Gernsback, stressed the relationship to science, especially technological innovation, while others, such as Frederik Pohl, were equally interested in exploring social and cultural change. Consequently, 'hard sf' took its meaning by differentiating itself from 'soft sf', a term used to describe works extrapolated not from natural but social sciences, such as anthropology, psychology or linguistics.

Sf that emphasises new technologies, disregarding their entanglement in the social

Throughout their history, 'hard' and 'soft' sf have carried gendered connotations, with hardness evoking masculine strength and technological dominance, and softness implying a less rigorous approach to science and a feminine concern with the social realm and relationships. Sf more interested in, for example, the psychological effects of technologies – a theme central to J.G. Ballard – is often associated with women's contributions to the field. But as Ballard demonstrates, the gendering of concepts does not neatly map onto an author's gender identity.

The idea of 'hard sf' is sometimes evoked to privilege forms of sf that emphasise new technologies or scientific discussions, while understating or disregarding their entanglement in the social realm. Such sf is sometimes described as not having a politics, usually by those who assert that 'real' sf should be about science, while failing to recognise that such a position is itself deeply political.

This way of framing the matter is analogous to the some-times-contentious relationship between science practice and science studies. The latter refers to a range of interdisciplinary approaches that study the history, cultural politics, regional variation and social consequences of science and technology. As science studies points out, the boundary between what is science and what is pseudoscience – like that between 'hard' and 'soft' sciences – changes historically and geographically. For example, telepathy, dear to much sf, was once an object of serious scientific study but is now regarded as entirely fictional. Moreover, as theories of decolonisation within science stud-ies explain, non-Western cultures often articulate and practice science in ways that are not legible as science within Western frameworks, but nonetheless create knowledge about the same natural world phenomena.

The idea of 'hard sf' only has meaning as part of these related and unstable binary oppositions. And, in any case, it is difficult nowadays to find sf extrapolating from science without also considering social, cultural, economic or political contexts or changes.

Hard sf

- ◘ Gwyneth Jones, *Proof of Concept* (2017)
- ◘ Peter Watts, *Blindsight* (2006)*
- ◘ David G. Hartwell and Kathryn Cramer, eds, *The Hard Sf Renaissance* (2002)
- ◘ Ted Chiang, *Stories of Your Life and Others* (2002)
- ◘ Greg Egan, *Luminous* (1998)

Onscreen hard sf

- ◘ *The Martian* (Scott 2015)
- ◘ *Interstellar* (Nolan 2014)
- ◘ *Primer* (Carruth 2004)
- ◘ *2001: A Space Odyssey* (Kubrick 1968)*
- ◘ *Destination Moon* (Pichel 1950)

SHERRYL VINT

Follow the science. Imagine what is possible.

A complex vision of plants as active and communicative beings

Semiosis extrapolates thoroughly and carefully from contemporary knowledge in natural sciences while at the same time deeply engaging with frameworks central to the social sciences. Along with its sequel, *Interference* (2019), it follows the first several generations of a group of colonists who left Earth so as to withdraw from a human culture consumed by war, exploitation and environmental destruction. They establish a new Pax constitution on the planet they settle, believing it to have no other sentient species.

As it tells the story of the original colonists and their descendants, *Semiosis* addresses questions of social and political change. This includes the gulf between the first generation who, traumatised by their experience on Earth, idealise their colonial initiative, and a generation born into the difficulties of trying to begin subsistence agriculture on unfamiliar terrain. At the same time, however, the novel is an exemplar of the style of plausible scientific extrapolation valued by hard sf's advocates. The expedition carefully picks its members for their disciplinary expertise – chemists, botanists, experts in medicine and animal husbandry – and there are numerous scenes of these people discussing how best to achieve their goals. Other scenes follow one or another character into the minutiae of their discipline and practice as they try to solve a specific scientific problem.

The most important science from which Burke builds her narrative is botany, a discipline the genre has not privileged as frequently as physics or astronomy. She generalises from recent discussions about chemical signals through which plants communicate with one another and shape their environments – to repel insects, for example, or redistribute nutrients – in order to posit a planet on which evolution diverged from its terrestrial path, resulting in plants rather than animals as the dominant lifeform. At first the colonists are blind to this possibility because it is too far outside the scientific assumptions they bring with them, an apt illustration of science-in-action that demonstrates that sometimes it is necessary to change default assumptions about how nature functions in order to make sense of the data one accumulates.

Utilising sf's capacity to narrate from non-human perspectives, Burke writes some of the duology from the point of view of the planet's apex plant species. It struggles to make sense of the humans and eventually to communicate with them, just as they work to understand the ecosystem and establish a relationship with the plant. The novel beautifully demonstrates that a radically different ethical context demanding new ways of living as humans can be prompted as much by the 'hard' as by the 'soft' sciences. In addition to asking us to think more capaciously about plants (as well as animals) when we think about ecology, *Semiosis* educates us in a complex vision of plants as active and communicative beings, updating our understanding in line with recent botanical research that belies earlier assumptions about the passivity and silence of plants.

Aniara (Pella Kågerman and Hugo Lilja 2018)

Some rules cannot be broken. Put enough CO_2 into the atmosphere, the Earth burns. Mars cannot be made that habitable. And if a spaceship fleeing one world for the other goes off course without fuel, there's no turning back, no tech solution, just inertia, cold equations, a slow-burn *High-Rise*, silence.

→ | Latinx futurisms

TARYNE JADE TAYLOR

Decolonise your mind
– and sf – with sf.

Latinx futurisms use speculative fiction as a method of decolonisation. They present Latinx and people of colour in imagined futures from which mainstream sf typically erases them, and reflect on what it means to be Latinx in the diaspora, reclaiming and repurposing an identity category often rife with stereotypes. For example, in *Sleep Dealer* (Rivera 2008), all the principal characters are Latinx, but some face internalised colonisation and racism. They each re-evaluate their identity, prompting viewers to examine the deleterious stereotypes they might themselves hold.

Latinx speculative fiction often plays with the idea of alienation, drawing on the stereotype of Latinxs as distanced from a technologically advanced future *and* the language of Latinx border crossers into the US who are officially labelled as 'resident' or 'illegal' aliens. *Sleep Dealer*'s decolonial critique of the way Western science and technology are privileged over Indigenous science and traditional technology frames Latinxs' engagement with new technologies. Centrally, milpa, the several thousand–year–old Indigenous agricultural technology, is contrasted with exploitative cyberpunk technologies extracting Latinx labour for American capitalism. Mexicans work as Cyberbraceros, remotely operating robot nannies and construction drones in a US they are not allowed to enter physically. In Rosaura Sánchez and Beatriz Pita's *Lunar Braceros 2125–2148* (2009), Latinxs forced to live in US reservations often become Moon Tecos, sent off-world to dispose of Earth's trash, with no hope of return.

Latinx futurisms show how the legacies of colonisation and exploitation create feelings of alienation. In the foreground of Chicana artist Laura Molina's painting *Amor Alien* (2004), a Latina, portrayed as a stereotypical green alien in a red bikini,

Remotely operating robot nannies and construction drones in a US they are not allowed to enter

sits on the lap of white astronaut Naked Dave, on a planet that is clearly not Earth. Addressing anti-immigrant, particularly anti-Mexican, sentiments in the US, it emphasises that it is not the Latina who is the alien. It reminds us that many Mexican Americans did not migrate to the US but rather that the US moved the border through violent conquest; it also acknowledges the Indigenous heritage of many Latinxs.

Latinx futurisms often work to redefine Latinxs away from a privileged white European look so as to celebrate the many other racialised peoples who make up the Americas and to contest colonial narratives and stereotypes of Latinx Americans as uncivilised and lacking technological savvy. In Sabrina Vourvoulias' *Ink* (2012), it is the Indigenous cosmological powers of the nahuals that build a better future. By representing Indigenous and African-based cosmologies and syncretised cosmologies, Latinx futurisms ask why Western science and cosmologies are privileged over them.

Latinx futurisms tie the present and future to the past by presenting decolonial pathways to a just future, but need not be set in the future. Zoraida Córdova's *Brooklyn Brujas* series (2016–18) and Daniel José Older's *Outlaw Saints* series (2022) draw on brujería and santería, respectively, as central parts of their world-building. Although they are YA urban fantasy rather than sf, they nonetheless presence Latinx characters in a better future through the traditional cosmologies that offer a path to it.

Latinx futurisms

- Alex Hernandez, Matthew David Goodwin and Sarah Rafael García, eds, *Speculative Fiction for Dreamers* (2021)
- Jennifer Givhan, *Trinity Sight* (2019)
- Carlos Hernandez, *The Assimilated Cuban's Guide to Quantum Santeria* (2016)
- Lilliam Rivera, *Dealing in Dreams* (2019)
- Frank Espinosa, *Rocketo* (2005–6)

Onscreen Latinx futurisms

- *Nuevo Rico* (Mercado 2021)
- *Alita: Battle Angel* (Rodriguez 2019)
- *Coco* (Unkrich and Molina 2017)
- *The Book of Life* (Gutiérrez 2014)
- *A Day without a Mexican* (Arau 2004)

TARYNE JADE TAYLOR

When the death god comes calling, what choice do you have?

Gods of Jade and Shadow is part of an emerging subset of Latinx futurisms called mesofuturisms, which includes David Bowles' *The Smoking Mirror* (2015),* J.C. Cervantes' *The Storm Runner* (2018),* Aiden Thomas' *Cemetery Boys* (2020) and Rebecca Roanhorse's *Black Sun* (2020).* Such fiction draws on Mesoamerican cosmologies as a central part of its world-building, thus countering the dominant canon of Anglophone sf and fantasy, which tends to utilise cosmologies from the Global North, particularly Greco-Roman, Celtic and Norse. Moreno-Garcia crafts a fantasy world steeped in Mesoamerican mythology, and her novel opens with a quote from The Popul Vuh, one of the most important surviving texts of the Maya. She champions the historically supressed Indigenous heritage of those of Mexican and Latin American descent in an effort to decolonise the psyches of her readers and the fantasy genre itself.

After her father's death, Casiopea Tun, the protagonist of *Gods of Jade and Shadow*, and her mother return to their native town in the Yucatan and join the household of her wealthy grandfather. However, because of Casiopea's dark skin and obvious Indigenous heritage, she is ostracised by her relatives. Throughout the novel, they exhibit anti-Indigenous sentiments and deny their own indigeneity. Valuing only their Spanish heritage, they treat Casiopea more like a maid than a family member. Their racism persists, even though they seek counsel from Maya Daykeepers, keepers of the 260-day calendar used to guide community values, and ritually travel to a cenote, a sacred sinkhole that typically includes a large pool of water and a cave system, to avail themselves of its healing properties. Through Casiopea's grandfather and cousin, Moreno-Garcia

It is also a journey of internal decolonisation

underscores the hypocrisy of anti-Indigenous sentiments in Latin America, especially when Casiopea learns of her family's connection to the death god Hun-Kamé. Once the ruler of Xibalba, the Mayan underworld, he embroils Casiopea in his supernatural schemes to dethrone his usurping twin brother, Vucub-Kamé. Together, they travel to Veracruz, Mexico City, El Paso and Baja California. For Casiopea, it is also a journey of internal decolonisation.

Moreno-Garcia's cross-hatched setting of jazz-age Mexico and Xibalba counters the rhetoric often used to legitimise the imperial projects of the Global North, not least its stereotyping of Mexico and Latin America as uncivilised places. She depicts Mexico City as a rival to major European and US cities and in no way their inferior, and shows the Maya gods and the past civilisations of Mexico surpassing modernity in many ways. Her Mesoamerican-inspired world-building upends stereotypes not only about Mexico's past, but also about the future, decolonising the history of Mexicans and the Mexican diaspora and paving a way for a decolonial future.

***Sleep Dealer* (Rivera 2008)**

A hacker from Oaxaca, running from disaster and towards maquilador exploitation. A Chicana wannabe journalist fleeing student loans. A Chicano pilot, second-generation US military, appalled by what he has done. With this rebel alliance against neoliberal Empire, the Global South finds its own use for cyberpunk things.

→ | Neurodiversity

DAVID HARTLEY

We're all wired differently. It's a feature, not a bug.

If sf is the genre of 'cognitive estrangement', might that also make it 'neurodivergent'?

A recent increase in the diagnoses of cognitive conditions, such as autism, ADHD, OCD and dyslexia, has led to the formation of communities who see these neurological differences as less a pathological affliction and more a fundamental part of identity. In *Odd People In* (1998), Judy Singer coined the term 'neurodiversity' to describe the idea that variation in neurocognitive ability is entirely natural, and that so-called disorders may be better understood as minds that are just differently wired.

The cyberpunk phrasing here is no accident. The idea of neurodiversity supercharged an emerging activism among autistic individuals, many of whom were using the new online social arenas of the digital age to reconfigure their understanding of their condition. Running in contrast to the terror that surrounded autism in the wake of the 1998 MMR vaccine scare, these social hackers began to see the strengths and benefits of being neurodivergent, as well as the shortage of accessibility and understanding in a world designed for the neurotypical.

And while sf tropes of alien visitors and emotionless robots are often dehumanisingly employed to describe the neurodivergent, it is also not uncommon to find sf fandoms filled with those who find deep pleasures in escapist world-building, the nerdiness of detail and atypical ways of thinking and behaving. Many neurodivergent sf fans found kindred spirits among alien and cyborg heroes, such as *Star Trek*'s Spock and Data and *Doctor Who*'s the Doctor, while the worlds of Philip K. Dick and William Gibson offered new neuro-romances for those who felt cognitively estranged.

Less a pathological affliction and more a fundamental part of identity

The field of neurodiversity studies now seeks to make utopian strides towards a reformulation of all neurosocial paradigms, from schooling to employment to the care of the elderly and the cognitive alternatives of non-human animals. Autistic activist Remi Yergeau's *Authoring Autism* (2017) offers the 'neuroqueer' as a productive coupling which turns pathologised divergent behaviours into gestures of resistance against the oppressive ideals of the neuro-normative.

Neurodiversity permeates broadly, and sf can use its inclination towards divergent states to help fathom these new networks of cognitive possibility. Autistic authors, including Rivers Solomon, Corinne Duyvis and Dora Raymaker, place neurodivergent characters in traumatic futures where the value of neurological difference is tested and scrutinised while the oppressions of typicality are exposed. For example, in Elle McNicol's *Show Us Who You Are* (2021), lifelike holograms of the recently deceased are programmed with 'improvements' that rid them of their so-called disorders, much to the horror of her plucky autistic heroine. Rather differently, *Inside Out* (Docter and Del Carmen 2015) helps us to visualise natural inner neurodivergence as chemicals and experiences produce fluctuations in moods and memories.

For the neurodivergent, sf can offer a space where lived experience of real 'cognitive estrangement' is not wholly dismissed or demonised, but instead reflects back on the fallacies of typicality while highlighting the vitality and richness of neurodivergent futures.

Neurodiversity in sf

- Rivers Solomon, *An Unkindness of Ghosts* (2017)
- Corinne Duyvis, *On the Edge of Gone* (2016)
- Emma Newman, *Planetfall* (2015)*
- Elizabeth Moon, *Speed of Dark* (2002)
- Octavia E. Butler, *Parable of the Sower* (1993)*

Neurodiversity in screen sf

- *Marjorie Prime* (Almereyda 2017)
- *Rise of the Planet of the Apes* (Wyatt 2012)*
- *Robot & Frank* (Schreir 2012)
- *Pi* (Aronofksy 1998)
- *Cube* (Natali 1997)*

DAVID HARTLEY

A future world. A triple homicide. A neurodivergent detective.

Deep in the heart of her beloved Red City, private investigator Hoshi Archer prays to the holy trinity of Signal, Encoding, and Noise: the core elemental triad of the quantum powered Memspace that keeps the city operational. Only the Operators, like Hoshi, who have the visual-associative acuity that comes with their K-Syndrome can programme the Mem. But the trade-offs are disabling difficulties in sensory processing, motor coordination and linguistic ability. Worse still, when mitigating neural implants allow Operators to integrate into wider society, the normies do not welcome them with open arms. Which makes things extra difficult when Hoshi has a triple murder to solve. Hence her prayers.

K-Syndrome is modelled directly on the author's own autism, and she uses Hoshi as a way to explore the condition as a neuroqueer way of being and thinking. Under the pretext of being an unstable person with a disability, Hoshi must regularly report to an 'integration officer' to provide details on her routine activities. Has she eaten enough meals? Slept enough? Failure to meet her quotas will mean a return to Operational enslavement, and yet the same scrutiny is not applied to the neurotypicals of the strained and fractious city. K-Syndrome, much like autism, remains framed by a medical model where pity pairs with disgust, and exploitation comes in the guise of support.

De-integration reflects the eternal threat of institutionalisation, while the bureaucratic concern with meeting basic survival quotas will feel familiar to the neurodivergent of whom nothing greater is expected or desired.

The same scrutiny is not applied to the neurotypicals of the strained and fractious city

Hoshi, therefore, must make her own destiny, and the reader stays firmly inside her divergent neurology as she endeavours to protect her space. The neural implants enable the Operators to regulate sensory filters and redirect cognitive energies. They also help with generating the comparatively plodding verbal language of the normies, as well as appropriate facial expressions for social interaction. But rather than a posthumanist fantasy, this technology is forever in the service of making Operators appear 'normal', thus quelling neurotypicals' anxieties. Such pressures to pass can be as exhausting as they are demoralising for neurodivergent people, while the frequent glitches in Hoshi's tech capture the ever-present threat of overwhelm and meltdown.

But Hoshi does have her pleasures. Chief among them is Red City itself. As a calming technique, she runs through her catalogue of favourite buildings – a self-stimulation of sensory appreciation and real-world grounding. Furthermore, she is blessed by an apparent bug in her neural programming that grants her cloaked access to the city's sensors and data points. Useful, of course, for a detective story, but also deeply ironic: Hoshi is the city whose society does not want her. This renders neurodivergence ubiquitous; it is the very fabric of signal, encoding and noise in both the real and virtual spaces.

Hoshi and the Red City Circuit demonstrates that without the cognitively estranged, we cannot imaginatively speculate.

***Everything Everywhere All at Once* (Daniel Kwan and Daniel Scheinert 2021)**

Sometimes it's all too much. Family, work, middle age, taxes, the dislocation of leaving one country, the disappointments of living in another. And then there's the multiverse. Infinite iterations of you and your life: dazzling, absurd, chaotic, headlong. Like ADHD, but with added kung fu.

HUGH C. O'CONNELL

After the struggle for liberation, what can be recovered? And what must change?

Sf's origins are inextricably linked to the sociopolitical context of imperialism. From 'lost race' novels, like H. Rider Haggard's *King Solomon's Mines* (1885), and tales of colonial blowback, like H.G. Wells' *The War of the Worlds* (1897), to the explorations of uncharted realms in Jules Verne's *Voyages extraordinaires* (1863–1919), early sf is suffused with the imperial imaginary. Such tales of external cultures encountering supposedly less technologically advanced societies presented opportunities for mediating the political and ethical ramifications of European imperialism. They ran the gamut of colonial attitudes – offering defences, recriminations and ambiguous portrayals – but still typically foregrounded and defined European culture over and against colonised Others.

Postcolonial sf complicates and reverses these colonial points of view. It recovers marginalised histories, reverses the colonial gaze and recasts first-contact narratives as instances of second contact so as to highlight the pervasive disruptions of the colonial encounter. It also blurs genre, bringing multiple fantastic and speculative modes together.

By retelling Indigenous histories as modes of historical, intellectual and cultural decolonisation, postcolonial sf imagines new political possibilities. This often takes the form of intervening in histories occluded or whitewashed by colonial narratives. For example, Nisi Shawl's alternate history *Everfair* (2016) provides a steampunk revisioning of the Belgian colony of the Congo Free State. Amitav Ghosh's *The Calcutta Chromosome* (1995) reimagines history by recounting the discovery of the vector for malaria from the point of view of unnamed Indian workers, leading to fantastic discoveries undreamt of by the colonisers. Both novels also draw on real historical figures to retell

To decentre the West's claim to be the only site and progenitor of futurity

the movement from colonisation through independence and into their speculative futures. Moreover, they simultaneously critique and recast dominant tropes within sf as well, including steampunk's often overly cosy portrayals of imperialism and sf's reliance on Enlightenment-cum-imperial notions of empirical mastery.

In this way, postcolonial sf often critiques typical sf narrative protocols and novums before salvaging them to reverse the discursive power of the colonial gaze and instead foreground Indigenous perspectives. Ultimately, this underscores postcolonial sf's desire to decentre the West's claim to be the only site and progenitor of futurity. If Western modernity – a product of the imperial accumulation by dispossession of wealth, labour power and resources from the colonies to the metropole – locked non-Western cultures outside of history and the future, postcolonial sf is imbued with a utopian impulse to recover possibilities and develop new futurities.

Such undercutting of imperial mastery and dominance, typically figured through superior technological development and Enlightenment mastery, finds its corollary in postcolonial sf's blending of genres. Elements of sf, fantasy and horror and/or Indigenous folklore, mythology and religion sit side by side. This centring of non-Western cultures, knowledges and ways of being brings new possibilities to the forefront of the sf imagination and undermines Western instrumentalised notions of rationality.

Postcolonial sf

- ◼ Priya Sarukkai Chabria, *Clone* (2019)
- ◼ Andrea Hairston, *Will Do Magic for Small Change* (2016)*
- ◼ Ngũgĩ wa Thiong'o, *Wizard of the Crow* (2006)
- ◼ Kojo Laing, *Major Gentl and the Achimota Wars* (1992)
- ◼ Sony Labou Tansi, *Life and a Half* (1979)

Postcolonial screen sf

- ◼ In the Future, *They Ate from the Finest Porcelain* (Lind and Sansour 2015)
- ◼ *Africa Paradis* (Amoussou 2006)
- ◼ *Les Saignantes* (Bekolo 2005)
- ◼ *Bedwin Hacker* (El Fani 2003)
- ◼ *The Quiet Earth* (Murphy 1985)

→ | Namwali Serpell, *The Old Drift* (2019)

HUGH C. O'CONNELL

Edging into the future from a broken, unstable past.

Serpell's critically lauded debut novel won not only the Arthur C. Clarke Award, but also the Belles-Lettres Grand Prix des Associations Littéraires, the *L.A. Times*' Art Seidenbaum Award for First Fiction and the Anisfield-Wolf Book Prize for fiction 'that confronts racism and explores diversity'. In this, it is similar to such other well-known postcolonial sf texts as Salman Rushdie's *Grimus* (1975), Buchi Emecheta's *The Rape of Shavi* (1983) and Amitav Ghosh's *The Calcutta Chromosome* (1995) in its ability to seamlessly court readers of both genre and literary fiction. Its narrative couples a lyrically rich magical realism with aspects of the historical novel (including many real figures and events), alongside sf investigations of bleeding-edge technologies like nanotech drones, biotech and computing, to re-explore the history of Zambia's colonisation and independence and its possible futures.

Split into three parts, *The Old Drift* is a sweeping multigenerational and national epic that moves from 1904 to 2024. It covers the intertwined lives of three families – white, brown and black – and examines colonialism's brutal racism, the socialist roots of independence movements and the corrupt post-independence government's complicity in furthering neo-imperial underdevelopment as economic globalisation entangled and engulfed the newly postcolonial nation. At stake, then, are a set of familiar postcolonial sf questions. How does the past inform the future? If sf is not only commensurate with but also conditioned by the logic of imperialism, how can we revitalise its narrative protocols towards anti-colonial liberation? If the answer to the end of imperialism was the neo-imperialism of global capitalism, how can we imagine a future that acknowledges these structural limits while seeking to break free from these geopolitical confines?

To decolonise not only the genre but the future itself

Among the novel's many rich narrative veins, the sections that will likely prove most rewarding for the reader interested in exploring postcolonial sf's animating questions can be found in the novel's latter parts. In ways that could draw parallels to Deji Bryce Olukotun's *Nigerians in Space* (2014) and *After the Flare* (2017), the second part revisits the 1960s Zambian Afronaut programme, little remembered today aside from a few derisive accounts in Western media. Serpell presents it as a 'double vision' that 'blended together science and fable, African technology and Western philosophy' (167). This strand of the narrative not only decentres the sf imaginary of space as the final (colonial) frontier, recalling Cecil Rhodes' ultimate ambition 'to annex the planets if I could', but also reimagines the programme as a ploy to capture Western investments that could then be redeployed towards Zambia's anti-colonial revolution. The third part, which intertwines the search for a cure for AIDS with the development of high-tech digital implants and nano-drone technology, strikes a similar anti-neo-imperial note. By decentring Western narratives of futurity, it – and the novel as a whole – pursues postcolonial sf's vocation to decolonise not only the genre but the future itself.

> ### *Crumbs* (Miguel Llansó 2015)
>
> After the end of our history, Candy and Sayat make a life in our ruins, our petrocultural detritus, our leftover images. Candy follows the route of colonial extraction, along our trainlines from our long-abandoned mines down to our ports. We are long gone, but somehow we have still not left.

CHRIS PAK

We are not separate and distinct. We are entangled, all the way down.

Posthumanism challenges and reimagines the philosophical status of the human. It imagines new forms of embodiment, including technological adaptations of the body through cyborgisation, genetic engineering and the conversion and uploading of consciousness into virtual reality. Posthuman hybrids disrupt the boundaries between the technological, the animal and the human, and trouble the notion that we are coherent, independent subjects.

Donna Haraway's influential 'A Cyborg Manifesto' (1991) demonstrates how contemporary existence is thoroughly shaped by the convergence of machine and organism. N. Katherine Hayles' *How We Became Posthuman* (1999) traces the twentieth-century development of cybernetics and computing technology that made possible the emergence of posthuman perspectives. More recently, Nick Bostrom's 'Transhumanist Values' (2005) and Humanity+'s 'Transhumanist Declaration' (2009) advocate for the technologically directed evolution of the human, arguing it is both necessary and inevitable.

In contrast to transhumanism, which focuses on the future embodied status of humankind, 'critical posthumanism', exemplified by Rosi Braidotti's *Posthuman Knowledge* (2019), challenges humanist and anthropocentric models of the human subject as unitary, stable and rooted in rational thought. For the critical posthumanist, transhumanism does not represent a radically new conception of the human so much as it extends the humanist subject into the future. As Cary Wolfe's *What Is Posthumanism?* (2010) argues, at the root of the humanist subject is the distinction between the human and non-human animal. Historically, this binary empowered colonialism: it enabled colonisers to exclude many peoples from being considered human. In the same way, it validated the exclusionary treatment of women and the working class.

The human subject has always been open to revision

The notion of a stable and universal human identity is thus ethnocentric and androcentric. It has been challenged by anti-colonialism, postcolonialism, feminisms, the environmental humanities and disability studies, all of which demonstrate how the human subject has always been open to revision. Critical posthumanism is therefore anti-essentialist. It refuses the idea that the human is defined by some eternal essence, and it deconstructs hierarchical conceptions of the human.

While embodiment is key for posthumanism, recognition of the non-human networks in which we are biologically, socially and technologically embedded further destabilises the notion that hard boundaries separate these categories. This insight underpins posthumanist challenges to anthropocentric views of the human subject. For example, Haraway's *When Species Meet* (2008) shows how humans are implicated in wider networks involving other animals and socio-technological systems, which upsets the idea that humans are bounded, autonomous subjects. If we take seriously the relationships among human and non-human actors, and the ways in which they mutually constitute each other in specific contexts, we can begin to re-conceptualise the networks that give shape to the identities of those so entangled. Hence, in *Staying with the Trouble* (2016), Haraway rejects the term 'posthuman' in favour of envisioning entanglements as a kind of posthuman compost. By doing so, she acknowledges the multiplicity of identities entangled with one another, and emphasises the need to cultivate the ability to respond appropriately to all those actors, human and otherwise, implicated in and constructed by the network.

Posthumanist sf

- Justina Robson, *Natural History* (2003)*
- Eva Hoffman, *The Secret* (2002)
- Nancy Kress, *Beggars in Spain* (1993)*
- Geoff Ryman, *The Child Garden* (1989)
- Bruce Sterling, *Schismatrix* (1985)

Posthumanist screen sf

- *The Congress* (Folman 2013)
- *Moon* (Jones 2009)
- *Ghost in the Shell* (Oshii 1995)*
- *Tetsuo* (Tsukamoto 1989)*
- *Videodrome* (Cronenberg 1983)

CHRIS PAK

Hybrids. Hybrids. Hybrids. Networks. Networks. Networks.

Set in Nigeria, primarily in 2066, *Rosewater* follows Kaaro, a powerful 'sensitive' recruited by the clandestine government agency S45. The city of Rosewater grew around the alien Wormwood, a colony of organisms with distributed agency and cognition. Wormwood transforms life, allowing Kaaro and others to access a communal information system known as the xenosphere, thus enabling mind reading and the manipulation of sensations and perception. The ubiquitous xenoforms, a biological network analogous to mycelia, bond with humans to connect them to the xenosphere.

As human-alien symbionts, sensitives trouble the unitary, stable human subject whose supposed boundaries separate individuals from the external world and other lifeforms. Moreover, their plasticity produces variegated and shifting forms that disrupt any sense of the body as unified and coherent. And the fact that sensitives can connect 'telepathically' through the xenosphere to access others' thoughts undermines the notion of a hard bodily boundary and invites us to recognise the ways in which the human is implicated in a network of animal and alien others. 'How human am I?' Kaaro wonders (358), even as the novel prompts the reader to ask, what does 'human' even mean anymore?

The ubiquity of tech implants challenges the biological-technological boundary. Phone implants are unremarkable, even when combined with augmented-reality interfaces. Radiofrequency identification implants are prevalent and an important tool for state control. Perhaps the clearest expression of the posthuman is the Machinery, a movement that argues the 'human body [can] best [be] conceptualised as a machine' (203). This emphasis on functionalism, and on expunging behaviours that traditionally constitute ideas of humanity, expresses the

A colony of organisms with distributed agency and cognition

transhumanist desire for a 'higher form of humanity' (203).

At the same time, however, Rosewater connects its (post) humanist explorations to colonialism. Ryan Miller, the 'ghost' or simulation of a seventeenth-century priest, resides as a pattern, an informational entity, in the xenosphere. Anarchist revolutionary Oyin Da explicitly connects Wormwood's colonisation of Nigeria and Britain's colonisation of West Africa. The US closes its borders and completely withdraws from international interactions as 'a way for America to stay human' (386), thus excluding the rest of the world from that category. Meanwhile, the sensitives are positioned as both more and less than human, and Wormwood's increasing hybridisation of human subjects is presented as both colonial appropriation and the erasure of human subjectivity.

Contrasting the xenobiological and technological creates the possibility of imagining posthuman existence in terms other than those established by the cyborg. Connectivity through the xenosphere resemble sf's imagination of virtual space. Communicating via viruses suggest another way of thinking about how hybridity works, although Thompson tends to use the language of cybernetics to describe the sensitives' experience. This interplay of the novel and the familiar suggests how difficult it has already become to conceptualise posthuman existences that are not informed by computing technologies. Yet the xenosphere also connects the bodily and virtual in ways that go beyond transhumanist visions of uploading consciousness into information space and of leaving the body behind.

Crimes of the Future (David Cronenberg 2022)

We are always already becoming other. Beneath the surface, our bodies are in rebellion, as much chaos as order, and evolution is an endless insurgency. What would it take for us to be at home in this world we have ruined? What new organs must emerge? What politics? What erotics?

→ Queer sf

KATIE STONE

Nothing is as 'natural' as you might think.

One of sf's key strengths is its capacity for taking that which is presented as natural and revealing it to be strange. It follows, then, that those elements of life most frequently and firmly tied to 'human nature' – sexual desire, gender identity, familial ties – would come under scrutiny. As early as 1818, Mary Shelley deployed the estranging effects of technology to destabilise the supposedly essential link between heterosexuality and reproduction. Frankenstein's experiments, and the many subsequent cyborg creations they inspired, demonstrate that baby making is as legitimate a subject of speculation as time travel or alien contact. Indeed, to read from a queer perspective is to recognise that any alien or futuristic civilisation encountered in the genre comes with its own gender system, its own method of reproduction, its own efforts to structure or police desire.

This is not to say that alien and cyborg sexualities are necessarily queer. As Susan Stryker notes, the notion that queer people are strange, alien or monstrous is frequently deployed by homophobes. When Stryker likens her experience as a trans woman to that of Frankenstein's Creature, she therefore does so in the knowledge that this affinity may well be used against her. But rather than attempting to assimilate into a transphobic society whose understanding of nature is designed to exclude her, she risks embracing her position as a consciously unnatural creation, utilising science-fictional strangeness within a queer politics of resistance.

Queer sf redefines what it might mean to have sex, to reproduce, to feel desire

In this context, it is useful to label, say, the vampiric aliens in Octavia E. Butler's *Fledgling* (2005), who feed erotically on humans regardless of gender, as 'queer'. By exploring sexual relationships which defy the dominant model of heterosexual monogamy, queer sf redefines what it might mean to have sex, to reproduce, to feel desire. From the affectionate nose touching of

Madeleine Olnek's codependent lesbian aliens to the recreation of self as alien in the work of visual art duo Materies Fecales, queer sf demonstrates that cisgender heterosex is but one option among many.

These queer possibilities are not foreclosed when sf focuses on human characters. In Nalo Hopkinson's fiction, for example, humans are just as likely as aliens to be queer. *The Salt Roads* (2003) highlights the vast array of different relationship structures in human history, from the love affairs of fourth-century Egyptian sex workers to the unrecognised marriages of enslaved communities in eighteenth-century Haiti. By doing so, Hopkinson demonstrates that the notion that heterosexuality is a universally accepted and homogenous human practice is predicated on the colonial erasure of queer lives – an erasure which has frequently stretched beyond our reality and into the strange worlds of sf.

To reclaim the connection between the queer and the alien, the strange or the monstrous is a subversive act that expands the boundaries of sf and of queer politics.

Queer sf

- Gretchen Felker-Martin, *Manhunt* (2022)
- Isabel Waidner, *Sterling Karat Gold* (2021)
- Akwaeke Emezi, *Freshwater* (2018)
- Samuel R. Delany, *Through the Valley of the Nest of Spiders* (2012)
- Maureen F. McHugh, *China Mountain Zhang* (1992)

Queer screen sf

- *The Sticky Fingers of Time* (Brougher 1997)
- *Poison* (Haynes 1991)
- *The Rocky Horror Picture Show* (Sharman 1975)*
- *Flesh for Frankenstein* (Morrisey and Margheriti 1973)
- *The Bride of Frankenstein* (Whale 1935)*

Rivers Solomon with Daveed Diggs, William Hudson and Jonathan Snipes, *The Deep* (2019)

KATIE STONE

Down below, something stirs. Something queer.

During the Middle Passage, enslaved African peoples lived under the threat of being thrown overboard by their European captors. *The Deep* – building on material from tracks by techno-electro duo Drexciya and hip-hop group clipping. – tells the story of the descendants of those who were pregnant when this threat was carried out, imagining a science-fictional afterlife for the children, born into terrifying waters, who had to learn to breathe beneath the waves. In what editor Navah Wolfe describes as a game of artistic telephone, Solomon has taken up the mythology of these mer-people, naming them wajinru or 'chorus of the deep', to tell a tale of traumatic memory, interspecies solidarity and collective resistance.

In this novella, Solomon explores the queer possibilities of cyborg bodies, part human and part something new. Each wajinru has the ability to gestate children and to impregnate sexual partners, and neither gender nor sexual preferences are presumed to be determined by their bodies. Wajinru live as men, women and nonbinary people, engaging in whatever sex acts they desire, with no pressure to conform to a reproductive norm. Protagonist Yetu is confused when humans use 'to couple' to mean sex as, for wajinru, sex can as easily take place in a group as between two people. Her own primary romantic interest is a human woman, meaning desire does not end at the borders of the wajinru community.

The queer possibilities of cyborg bodies, part human and part something new

However, this apparent utopia, where sexuality is self-determined and driven only by desire, is complicated in Solomon's telling. By situating the wajinru's sexual practices within the context of the Middle Passage and its legacies, Solomon demonstrates that sexuality does not exist within a vacuum. As Black feminist theorist Hortense Spillers argues, white supremacism has always presented the sexuality and reproductive capacities of Black people as perverted, whether they fit into the bracket of heterosexuality or not. People birthing children as they drown do not enjoy the advantages presumed common to all mothers within a heteronormative society. The queerness of the wajinru is, therefore, less a subversive alternative to the conformity of human society and more the ongoing sexual expression of a people who never fitted into the norms of dominant white culture.

The wajinru conception of sexual reproduction must also be considered in relation to the non-human world. After their mothers' deaths, the first wajinru were adopted into whale pods. The young wajinru feed on whale milk and learn the ways of the sea alongside these second mothers, thus rewriting the borders of the family to include non-human life. While many queer sf creators have viewed the natural world as a site of domination, Solomon reveals queer possibilities to be found among our non-human fellows. Rather than establishing the wajinru as a queer, alien exception to the rest of human and animal life, *The Deep* shows that nature was queer all along.

***Codependent Lesbian Space Alien Seeks Same* (Madeleine Olnek 2011)**

Because, perhaps, numbness, apathy and sadness are not the goal. Because, perhaps, everyone is a freak and an oddity in some context. Because, perhaps, the only universals are love, heartbreak, social awkwardness and the complex feelings aroused by doughnuts and cheesecake.

DAVID M. HIGGINS

Replaying – and rethinking – colonialism across a sea of stars.

There is no single authoritative definition of space opera, but you know it when you see it. The scale is vast, and the story – featuring rockets, robots, ray guns, space battles, larger-than-life heroes – may well go on forever, spawning sequels, spin-offs, even entire franchises.

The term was coined in 1941 by Wilson 'Bob' Tucker in his fanzine *Le Zombie* to describe the 'hacky, grinding, stinking, outworn' space adventure tales that frequently appeared in sf pulps in the 1920s and 1930s and were becoming common in other media, thanks to the success of Philip Francis Nowlan's *Buck Rogers* (from 1929) and Alex Raymond's *Flash Gordon* (from 1934) syndicated newspaper comic strips.

Tucker's pejorative usage was not meant to describe the stories now regarded as space opera's key progenitors, such as E.E. 'Doc' Smith and Lee Hawkins Garby's *The Skylark of Space* (1928),* Edmond Hamilton's *Interstellar Patrol* stories (1928–30) and C.L. Moore's weird science fantasy tales, or such major examples from the following decades as Smith's *Lensman* series (1937–54), A.E. van Vogt's *The Voyage of the Space Beagle* (1939–50), Isaac Asimov's *Foundation* series (1942–53) and Leigh Brackett's 'The Sea Kings of Mars' (1949). Instead, Tucker's 'space opera' referred to what he considered the trashy, juvenile and commercially successful adventures in outer space published in the likes of *Planet Stories*. For him, space opera was shallow, depthless popular entertainment – like 'soap operas', the serialised radio melodramas intended for housewives and sponsored by soap manufacturers, and 'horse operas', the equally formulaic radio Westerns. Indeed, before the late 1960s, no self-respecting sf writer would deliberately set out to write space opera other than as pastiche or parody, as in Alfred

Rockets, robots, ray guns, space battles, larger-than-life heroes

Bester's *The Stars My Destination* (1956) or Harry Harrison's *The Stainless Steel Rat* (1961).*

However, in the 1960s and 1970s, many began to look back at early space adventure stories from a broader vantage, and to realise that the value of Tucker's terminology lay not in his dismissal of some sf as popular trash but in his insight that many early sf stories were essentially 'horse operas' in space. Sf, in other words, often reproduced the tropes of popular settler-colonial adventure narratives, replacing colonial settings and indigenous peoples with distant planets and bug-eyed aliens. Such stories could be jingoistic in the extreme, as in Robert A. Heinlein's *Starship Troopers* (1959), but sf also satirised and critiqued these attitudes; Harrison's *Bill, the Galactic Hero* (1964)* and Joe Haldeman's *The Forever War* (1974)* respond directly to Heinlein, while *Starship Troopers* (Verhoeven 1997)* systematically refutes the novel it adapts.

Increasingly, highbrow and lowbrow space operas alike consciously redress early sf's unthinking celebration of settler colonialism, and newer space operas tend to explicitly problematise Euro-American imperialism. Indeed, a critique of empire is arguably the central characteristics of most noteworthy space operas since the 1960s, including Ursula K. Le Guin's *Hainish* stories (1966–2017), Joanna Russ' *Alyx* stories (1967–74), Samuel R. Delany's *Nova* (1968), Iain M. Banks' *Culture* series (1987–2012) and Arkady Martine's *Teixcalaan* series (2019–21).

Space opera

- Charlie Jane Anders, *Victories Greater Than Death* (2021)*
- N.K. Jemisin and Jamal Campbell, *Far Sector* (2020–21)
- Valerie Valdes, *Chilling Effect* (2019)
- David G. Hartwell and Kathryn Cramer, eds, *The Space Opera Renaissance* (2006)
- Pierre Christin and Jean-Claude Mézières, *Valérian and Laureline* (1967–2010)

Onscreen space opera

- *Guardians of the Galaxy* (Gunn 2014)*
- *Battlestar Galactica* (2003–09)*
- *Firefly* (2002–03)*
- *Babylon 5* (1993–98)*
- *Star Wars* (Lucas 1977)*

DAVID M. HIGGINS

The Empire is not what it used to be.

Ann Leckie's space opera was the first novel to win the Nebula, Hugo and Arthur C. Clarke awards. Followed by *Ancillary Sword* (2014) and *Ancillary Mercy* (2015), it tells the story of a civil war unfolding in the interstellar Radch empire.

Radchaai starships contain sentient artificial intelligences that can occupy both onboard computer systems and cybernetically enhanced human bodies. These 'ancillaries' are the victims of prior annexations: when the Radch colonises a planet, a portion of the population is implanted with technologies that transform them into networked extensions of the ship's AI. They are then used as soldiers in future annexations. *Ancillary Justice* is narrated from the perspective of Breq, the last surviving ancillary of the military troop carrier *Justice of Toren*.

As the novel opens, the practice of creating ancillaries has been largely discontinued, and Radch expansion is grinding to a halt because of a disagreement occurring within Anaander Mianaai, the Radchaai emperor, who exists across a multitude of networked bodies. Over millennia, profound ideological disagreements over the ethics of imperial annexation have emerged within different versions of the emperor. This has resulted in a shadow war between reactionary factions of the emperor who believe annexations must continue for the economic prosperity of the empire, and progressive versions of the emperor who strive toward far-reaching reforms. Breq – seeking revenge upon Anaander for the murder of her favourite officer, Lieutenant Awn – exposes this hidden conflict, causing it to erupt into open warfare.

Profound ideological disagreements over the ethics of imperial annexation

Ancillary Justice was written while the US, following the 9/11 attacks, pursued devastating military action in the Middle East. This context informs Leckie's portrayal of the Radch's annexation of foreign territories to create a buffer zone that will keep the imperial homeland free from immigrants and uncontaminated by violence. Leckie also shows how the luxuries enjoyed by imperial elites depend upon the economic exploitation of subaltern populations, and how racial categories are enforced through the state's differentiation between citizens and noncitizens.

But perhaps the novel's most noteworthy aspect is its treatment of gender identity and gender relations. Narrated from the perspective of an AI who largely regards gender as meaningless, it invites readers to imagine what gender might look like from an agender perspective – especially as Breq stumbles through misgendering people from alien cultures and using their pronouns incorrectly. On the one hand, this denaturalises the connections between biological sex and gender, showing gender to be the product of cultural norms. On the other, it exposes how coloniality informs the ways we experience gender. As an imperial soldier, Breq always interacts with people from other cultures from an asymmetrical position of power. One can only misuse people's pronouns without consequence if one occupies a social position that enables one to do so. *Ancillary Justice* thus demonstrates how power determines which attitudes towards gender carry weight and which can be neglected, ignored or dismissed.

Space Sweepers (Jo Sung-hee 2021)

Dying Earth. Terraformed Mars. Space elevators. Orbital megastructures. Edenic habitats for the rich. Space junk. A ragtag garbage crew. A nefarious genocidal tech bro. A girl who can save the planet. Killer robots. Nanotech. Polyglotism. Battles. Pursuits. Betrayals. Reversals. Melodrama. Sentiment. Implausibility. Cuteness. Bravery. Self-sacrifice. Solidarity. Scale. Colour. Kinesis. Velocity. Synaesthesia.

GLYN MORGAN

Can you beat the clock? Turn back time? Borrow it? Kill it?

We are all travelling in time. The fantasy of controlling that journey has long been a feature of the speculative imagination. In such time-slip narratives as Washington Irving's 'Rip Van Winkle' (1819) and Edward Bellamy's *Looking Backwards* (1888),* unconscious protagonists accidentally travel forward in time. But with Enrique Gaspar's *The Time Ship* (1887) and H.G. Wells' *The Time Machine* (1895), mechanical devices rendered time travel controllable and distinctly science-fictional, although the form these machines take varies considerably, from *Back to the Future*'s (Zemeckis 1985)* Delorean to the *Hot Tub Time Machine* (Pink 2010).*

From Albert Einstein's theory of general relativity, which explains that the faster you travel the more slowly you experience time, sf extrapolated a new mode of time travel. This time dilation effect allows space travellers approaching or exceeding the speed of light to make one-way trips into the future as less time passes for them than for those they leave behind, as in Stanisław Lem's *Return from the Stars* (1961), Ursula K. Le Guin's *Hainish Cycle* (1966–99), Joe Haldeman's *The Forever War* (1974)* and, perhaps most famously, as revealed at the end of *Planet of the Apes* (Schaffner 1968).*

Time dilation is a one-way trip. But if you could find a way to travel back from the future, what is to stop you travelling still further backwards into the past? Certain periods are popular destinations for time travel, including the Cretaceous in Robert J. Sawyer's *End of an Era* (1994) and the Second World War in Connie Willis' *Blackout* (2010).* Indeed, some events – such as the Crucifixion and Lincoln's assassination – are so popular that they might, as in Garry Kilworth's 'Let's Go to Golgotha!' (1975) and Karen Joy Fowler's 'Standing Room

Travelling into the past risks changing the future

Only' (1997), be packed with time tourists rather than locals. And sometimes, as in Michael Moorcock's *Behold the Man* (1969) and Tim Powers' *The Anubis Gates* (1983), the time traveller turns out to be the historical figure they wanted to meet.

Travelling into the past risks changing something and thus changing the future. In Ray Bradbury's 'A Sound of Thunder' (1952), the consequences of a prehistoric safari accidentally killing a butterfly propagate forward through time, radically altering the world. *Timecop* (Hyams 1994) features an organisation specifically dedicated to preserving the timeline by preventing the creation of alternate histories. Rival organisations can transform time into an arena for conflict, with 'time wars' or 'change wars' central to Jack Williamson's *The Legion of Time* (1938), Fritz Leiber's *The Big Time* (1958),* Stephen Baxter's *Time Ships* (1995) and the new iteration of *Doctor Who* (2005–).

However, not all time-travel stories relate to grand events or epic conflicts. Sometimes the focus is on intimate tales about personal lives, often including romance. Hence Yasutaka Tsutsui's *The Girl Who Leapt through Time* (1965–66), *Il Mare* (Lee 2000) and Audrey Niffenegger's *The Time Traveller's Wife* (2003) sit comfortably in sf alongside *The Terminator* (1984),* Hiroshi Sakuraza's *All You Need Is Kill* (2004) and Kameron Hurley's *The Light Brigade* (2019).

Time travel sf

- Amal El-Mohtar and Max Gladstone, *This Is How You Lose the Time War* (2019)
- Richard McGuire, *Here* (2014)
- Claire North, *The First Fifteen Lives of Harry August* (2014)
- Ann and Jeff VanderMeer, eds, *The Time Traveller's Almanac* (2013)
- Kathleen Ann Goonan, *In War Times** (2007)

Onscreen time travel

- *Beyond the Infinite Two Minutes* (Yamaguchi 2020)
- *Russian Doll* (2019–)
- *Day Break* (2006–07)
- *Je t'aime, je t'aime* (Resnais 1968)
- *La jetée* (Marker 1962)

GLYN MORGAN

Feminists versus incels.
Their battlefield: the timeline.

The Future of Another Timeline offers an original take on the time-travel narrative and a powerful, timely political message. It follows a group of time travellers who frequently journey into the past under the guise of research but with the secret intention of changing the timeline. They call themselves the 'Daughters of Harriet', after Harriet Tubman, who in one of the novel's timelines becomes a US senator in 1880. The Machines upon which they rely for time-travel wormholes are not human-constructed mechanisms but seemingly natural geological features at five known locations in the world. They will not allow a traveller to return to a time they have already visited, carry weapons or make major historical changes, and they will not open at all for anyone who has not remained within twenty kilometres of them for at least four years.

Unusually for sf, time travel is based in the university departments not of physics or engineering but of geology. The geoscientists among the Daughters of Harriet meet regularly to compare their recollections, never knowing what might have changed when they return from the past. Going around the circle, they recall events which occurred differently, laws which were passed or overturned, friends who no longer exist.

I remember abortion being legal in the United States

One memory in particular sums up both the troubling relevance of the novel and its central theme: 'I remember abortion being legal in the United States' (40). A few of the other Daughters share the same memory, or a version of it, which is uncommon and perhaps means 'the change to abortion's legal status was the product of multiple edits and reversions' (40). This early revelation introduces the main plot, a secret war between the Daughters of Harriet, who champion the rights of women and non-binary communities, and a group of angry young men known as the Comstockers. Of unknown origin, they take their name from Anthony Comstock, the infamous censor and so-called moralist. Both sides identify the late nineteenth century as a battlefield where the pattern for women's rights in the United States will be set for decades or centuries to come. Imbued with all of the venom and vitriol of twenty-first-century misogyny, the Comstockers echo the language of incels, men's rights groups and Donald Trump.

The Daughters and the Comstockers work in unofficial capacities, although, given the limited access to the Machines, they both must enjoy a certain level of tacit endorsement from somewhere in society. Their indirect warfare – making edits to the timeline to correct and allow for the edits of their adversaries – highlights the unsettled nature of history and how tenuous our supposed 'rights' are. Newitz's novel is a powerful reminder, if any were now needed, that the fight for progress is never settled: if the struggle stops, rights can be taken away far more easily than they were won.

Your Name **(Makoto Shinkai 2016)**

Adolescence is hard enough without your consciousness taking over someone else's body while you sleep, switching night for day, country for city, female for male – and theirs returning the favour. What if you fall in love with each other? If disaster approaches? If time is not on your side?

→ | Utopia

SARAH LOHMANN

There must be better ways of doing things.

Utopia might be defined as 'the verbal construction of a particular quasi-human community where sociopolitical institutions, norms, and individual relationships are organized according to a more perfect principle than in the author's community' (Suvin 63), but it remains more ambiguous than that.

With its roots in 'golden age' myths, utopia predates, but is also a subset of, sf. The term – a pun in Greek on 'no place' and 'good place' – was coined by Thomas More as the name of an imaginary island and the title of the book in which he describes it. As his playfulness suggests, perhaps utopia is most 'real' as an intellectual game or thought experiment. Indeed, classical utopias, such as Plato's *Republic* (ca. 370–360 BC) and More's *Utopia* (1516), are primarily explorations of abstract concepts (virtue and justice, respectively). However, abstraction also renders these societies static – inflexible models for contemplation rather than ideal societies for humans to inhabit.

Symbolic sanitised visions of perfection, partially influenced by monasticism, persisted. For example, Tommaso Campanella's *La Città del Sole (Civitas Solis)* (1602) describes a theocratic monarchy, and Johann Valentin Andreae's *Reipublicae Christianopolitanae Descriptio (Christianopolis)* (1619), a quasi-Lutheran workers' republic. But utopian novels soon became more interested in the worlds improved science and technology could create. Sir Francis Bacon's incomplete *New Atlantis* (1682) depicts a scientific society conquering nature, and, in the wake of the industrial and French revolutions, utopian novels took this belief in future-directed change even further. Edward Bellamy's *Looking Backward* (1888) and H.G. Wells' *A Modern Utopia* (1905) envisage technologically and socially improved futures – not elsewhere, but elsewhen. However, this temporal removal produces a certain sense of stasis, and in

The 'not-yet' of our deepest longings

these thought experiments inequalities persist and social function predominates over the individual.

By the mid-twentieth century, utopia was viewed far more sceptically. Technological optimism abruptly declined in the face of world wars, atomic bombs and genocides, and the desire to reshape society became associated with totalitarianism. But utopian hope survived: not in rigidly specified social constructs but, as Marxist philosopher Ernst Bloch argues, in the 'not-yet' of our deepest longings. Furthermore, the social justice movements of the 1960s and 1970s reawakened the literary utopia. Inspired by this revolutionary energy, Ursula K. Le Guin's *The Dispossessed* (1974), Joanna Russ' *The Female Man* (1975), Samuel R. Delany's *Triton* (1976) and Marge Piercy's *Woman on the Edge of Time* (1976) employed sf's imaginative potential to redesign utopia as an inclusive space of open-ended transformation.

Today, while the literary utopia has again all but disappeared, a victim perhaps of neoliberal cynicism and the difficulty of imagining an alternative to global capitalism, the utopian impulse is more alive than ever in collective mobilisations against climate change and in critical dystopias responding to this existential threat. For utopia works best when it draws on sf's estranging and transformative connections to the world. Utopia gives sf hope; sf grounds utopia in the possibilities of the real.

Utopias

- M.E. O'Brien and Eman Abdelhadi, *Everything for Everyone* (2022)
- Tim Maughan, *Infinite Detail* (2019)
- Hao Jingfang, *Vagabonds* (2016)
- Sarah Hall, *The Carhullan Army* (2007)
- Kim Stanley Robinson, *Red Mars* (1992)*

Onscreen utopias

- *The Good Place* (2016–20)
- *Star Trek* (1966–)*
- *Forbidden Planet* (Wilcox 1956)
- *Things to Come* (Menzies 1936)
- *Himmelskibet* (Holger-Madsen 1916)

SARAH LOHMANN

O brave new world that has such punks in't.

Sarah Pinsker's Nebula Award–winning debut novel is profoundly utopian despite its dystopian setting. Long after the terrorist attacks and a global pandemic that prompted them, laws forbidding humans to congregate are still in effect. Nearly all human interaction, including music performance, is relegated to the virtual sphere. Ernst Bloch contends that music is 'the most utopian of cultural forms, uniquely capable of conveying and effecting a better world' (Levitas 220), and in *A Song for a New Day* it is emblematic of both dystopian totalitarianism and utopian reinvention.

In traditional utopias, rulings about music tend to capture the extent of internal control such societies require in order to function, but in the 1970s critical utopias of Delany, Le Guin, Piercy and Russ, music is a creative liberatory communal ritual – a social polyphony in which music is utopia and utopia is music: immersive, ludic, harmonious and concerted. In *Song*, music is co-opted as a form of state control and survives as collective ritual. Like the drug soma in Aldous Huxley's dystopian *Brave New World* (1932), music is used to placate the masses and quell unrest, but music also holds the key to eventual liberation: a surviving punk-ish underground gigs behind shutters and in basements, waiting to break free.

> **Music is utopia and utopia is music: immersive, ludic, harmonious and concerted**

The novel has two protagonists. The younger, Rosemary, is a child of this new age. Growing up in isolation, she is fascinated by her first holographic concert. However, when she starts working for monopolising music distribution company StageHoloLive, she sees this virtual commodification of music for what it is: a mere simulacrum, a Baudrillardian perversion of the real, in which a glitch can cause a musician's images to 'crumple . . . like paper' (88). The older protagonist, Luce, shuns this hyperreal shadow world and cultivates an anarchist micro-utopia: in her small illegal performance space, live music remains alive.

The protagonists' trajectories intersect, old world against new, when Rosemary finds herself in Luce's venue trying to sign bands for StageHoloLive. Rosemary is delighted by the warmth of this community. She is 'a note that hadn't ever known it fit into a chord' (213), but she also represents a potentially catastrophic dystopian intrusion.

Pinsker, however, reframes disruption as a catalyst for change; as Luce says, 'live songs have teeth' that help 'spit ideas into the world' (63). Utopian energy resists absorption into state and corporate power, and from this dystopian crux utopia emerges. A tonal shift allows Rosemary and Luce, and the tendencies they represent, to harmonise.

Shortly before the novel's publication, Pinsker tweeted, 'This book is my attempt to make music in prose. . . . And hopefully tell a good SF story while I'm at it.' By highlighting the transformative power of utopian hope, especially in the face of adversity, she succeeded. When the night seems darkest, placing the creative transcendent communal alterity of music at the dawn of a possible new day reinvigorates utopia.

2040 (Damon Gameau 2019)

Existing technologies, bottom-up local energy grids, community-owned electric transport, regenerative agriculture, marine permaculture, science, good sense and doughnut economics could save the world from climate change *and* build a modest green middle-class liberal utopia for all in just twenty years. It's the hope that kills you.

→ | Weird

ROGER LUCKHURST

The filthy backwash of the sublime. Of something beyond.

'Weird' is rooted in the ancient languages of the north: Old English has 'weird' as a supernatural power over life's course, a fate, from Old Norse 'loop' or 'knot': a twist of fate. In the nineteenth century, it came to describe an uncanny feeling produced by texts such as Samuel Taylor Coleridge's *The Rime of the Ancient Mariner* (1798) that are 'weird' but not gothic. Weird became a generic marker late in the century, as in Charlotte Riddell's *Weird Stories* (1882). Rudyard Kipling often wrote weird stories from the edges of empire, but the Victorian and Edwardian writers most associated with the term are Arthur Machen and Algernon Blackwood.

Weird fiction found its place in the American pulps with *Weird Tales* magazine, first published in 1923, and now commonly associated with H. P. Lovecraft's stories and his definition: 'a certain atmosphere of breathless and unexplainable dread of outer, unknown forces'.

Inexplicable horrors, obtrusions glimpsed from other orders of existence

He emphasised the terror of the sublime, an unveiling of awful, annihilating truths: moments of *cosmic horror* that shatter complacent human confidence that they are the apex of evolutionary development. The mode peaked in the 1930s with Lovecraft, Robert Howard, Clark Ashton Smith and the novels of William Sloane, but lingered on in the work of, for example, Shirley Jackson, Nigel Kneale and Robert Aickman. In 2003, British writers M. John Harrison and China Miéville briefly toyed with the prospect of hailing a 'New Weird', but some American writers, notably Laird Barron and Caitlín R. Kiernan, ran with this neo-Lovecraftian revival, often working directly inside the Lovecraft mythos. The weird broke into mainstream publishing with Jeff VanderMeer's *Southern Reach* trilogy (2014), and has also been amenable to women writers, with Kelly Link, Karen Russell and Aliya Whiteley mining its quixotic seams.

The weird's other root is Shakespeare's punning 'weïrd' or 'weyard' sisters, the witches who either predetermine or manipulate Macbeth's actions. The weyard sisters are *wayward*, as is the genre of the weird: slippery, tangential, twisty, oozing outside neat definitional borders. Weird texts take unexpected turns, begin perhaps in a recognisable reality before breaching realist conventions and ushering in wild fantasy or inexplicable horrors, obtrusions glimpsed from other orders of existence. Writers in the tradition have been overlooked or declared minor because the weird falls somewhere outside the generic expectations of the gothic, the ghost story, sf and fantasy. The weird hovers on the edges of these forms, mutating regularly.

The weird dethrones the human, which makes it a highly political mode. For Lovecraft, displacement of white settler authority produced a reactionary horror of invasive threat, often racialised. The twenty-first-century revival, however, is less concerned with demonising monstrous others than with including the non-human. It has become a powerful method for exploring wholly other modes of animal existence, with much interest in octopi and other cephalopods. It provides a vehicle for transformative ecological thought and, through its abiding interest in fungal and viral life, for investigating entirely other modes of networked being.

Weird fiction

- Kij Johnson, *The Dream-Quest of Vellitt Boe* (2016)
- Ann and Jeff VanderMeer, eds, *The Weird* (2010)
- Mark Z. Danielewski, *House of Leaves* (2000)
- China Miéville, *Perdido Street Station* (2000)*
- M. John Harrison, *Signs of Life* (1997)

Onscreen weird

- *Fortitude* (2015–18)
- *Évolution* (Hadzihalilovic 2015)
- *The Last Winter* (Fessenden 2006)
- *Event Horizon* (Anderson 1997)
- *Stalker* (Tarkovksy 1979)

→ Caitlín R. Kiernan, *Agents of Dreamland* (2017)*

ROGER LUCKHURST

Reality thins. Time fragments. Something unutterable this way comes.

Caitlín R. Kiernan is a prolific writer of interstitial tales, novels and comics that are elusive, hard to define, suffused with Southern Gothic tonalities, best labelled 'weird'. A palaeontologist, with a specialism in dinosaurs, Kiernan's interest in deep geological time is evident in explicit borrowings from Lovecraft's mythos of the Old Ones, ancient monstrous beings pre-existing puny humanity. In a Lovecraftian manner, Kiernan generates glimpses of cosmic horror or sublimity amidst the outcasts surviving in the post-industrial rubble of late imperial America. Perhaps typical of the weird universe, Kiernan's pronouns have lately shifted from 'she' to 'they', refusing gender fixity for a more fluid condition.

Agents of Dreamland exists in a loose sequence, sharing characters with *Black Helicopters* (2013; revised and expanded 2018) and *The Tindalos Asset* (2020). Each of these novellas occupies and then remodels a central text from the weird tradition. In *Dreamland*, it is Lovecraft's 'The Whisperer in Darkness' (1931), but mixed with genre tropes from hard-boiled detective fiction, film noir and conspiracy thrillers, and laden with echoes of contemporary music, from Jimi Hendrix to the lesbian country-and-western star Mary Gauthier.

One of the best registers we have of the true state of things

There are allusions to the End Times envisaged in the Book of Revelations, and to real-life apocalyptic cults: Charles Manson's Family and Heaven's Gate, who in 1997 committed mass suicide to ascend to the stars. Kiernan's layering of references upon references makes for densely allusive and challenging stories, augmented further by their willingness constantly to revise, rewrite, extend and re-order the books between editions. This is a familiar weird tactic, a self-consciously bookish mode that tips a knowing wink to readers steeped in the tradition.

Kiernan picks up stories and gleefully shatters them into fragments (which often break off at hints of sublime terror or ecstasy). By scrambling the temporal sequence in this way, Kiernan forces the reader to work hard to establish cause and effect, while also deepening the sense that the sequential human time scale hides us from much larger, non-human, utterly alien rhythms and beings.

In *Agents of Dreamland*, the secret government agencies policing the borders of the paucity of our reality begin to suspect that the apocalyptic vision of a cult leader, whose followers have been engulfed and entirely transformed by a species of fungus, might link to a much larger cosmic story, which they cannot bear to comprehend. In this, the novella fulfils the quintessential weird experience, suggested in the opening paragraph of Lovecraft's 'The Call of Cthulhu' (1928), that 'some day the piecing together of dissociated knowledge will open up such terrifying vistas of reality, and of our frightful position therein, that we shall either go mad from the revelation or flee from the deadly light into the peace and safety of a new dark age'.

With our world teetering on the brink of disaster and our belated understanding of an apocalypse that has already begun to unfold, Kiernan's weird may be one of the best registers we have of the true state of things.

The Endless (Justin Benson and Aaron Moorhead 2017)

A UFO death cult in the California hills? A pre-digital, vaguely hipster, craft beer commune? Acolytes of a bad numinous, of some unseeable thing that watches from above? That distorts physics. That makes time ripple and eddy. That traps and enfolds. That never lets you go.

Bibliography

Allan, Kathryn. *Disability and Science Fiction: Technology as Cure*. Palgrave Macmillan, 2013.

Anzaldúa, Gloria. *Borderlands/La Frontera: The New Mestiza*. Aunt Lute Books, 1987.

Baccolini, Raffaella, and Tom Moylan. 'Introduction: Dystopia and Histories'. In *Dark Horizons: Science Fiction and the Dystopian Imagination*. Routledge, 2003, 1–12.

Berlatsky, Noah. 'Why Sci-Fi Keeps Imagining the Subjugation of White People'. *The Atlantic*, April 25, 2014. https://www.theatlantic.com/entertainment/archive/2014/04/why-sci-fi-keeps-imagining-the-enslavement-of-white-people/361173/.

Dery, Mark. 'Black to the Future: Interviews with Samuel R. Delany, Greg Tate, and Tricia Rose'. *Flame Wars: The Discourse of Cyberculture*, ed. Mark Dery. Duke University Press, 1994, 179–222.

Dillender, Kirsten. 'Land and Pessimistic Futures in African American Speculative Fiction'. *Extrapolation* 61, no. 1–2 (2020): 131–150.

Donawerth, Jane. 'Utopian Science: Contemporary Feminist Science Theory and Science Fiction by Women'. *NWSA Journal* 2, no. 4 (1994): 535–557.

Garforth, Lisa. 'Green Utopias: Beyond Apocalypse, Progress, and Pastoral'. *Utopian Studies* 16, no. 3 (2005): 393–427.

Gernsback, Hugo. 'A New Sort of Magazine'. *Amazing Stories* 1, no. 1 (April 1926): 3.

Haraway, Donna J. 'The Biopolitics of Postmodern Bodies: Constitutions of Self in Immune System Discourse'. In *Simians, Cyborgs and Women: The Reinvention of Nature*. Routledge, 1991, 203–230.

Haraway, Donna J. 'A Cyborg Manifesto: Science, Technology, and Socialist-Feminism in the Late Twentieth Century'. In *Simians, Cyborgs and Women: The Reinvention of Nature*. Routledge, 1992, 149–182.

Kafer, Alison. *Feminist, Queer, Crip*. Indiana University Press, 2013.

Levitas, Ruth. *The Privatization of Hope: Ernst Bloch and the Future of Utopia*. Duke University Press, 2013.

Mitchell, David, and Sharon Snyder. *Narrative Prosthesis: Disability and the Dependencies of Discourse*. University of Michigan Press, 2000.

Moylan, Tom. *Demand the Impossible: Science Fiction and the Utopian Imagination*. Peter Lang, 2014.

Neale, Stephen. *Genre*. London: BFI, 1980.

Plotz, John. 'The Realism of Our Times: Kim Stanley Robinson on How Science

Fiction Works'. *Public Books*, September 23, 2020. https://www.publicbooks.org/the-realism-of-our-times-kim-stanley-robinson-on-how-science-fiction-works/.

Sargent, Lyman Tower. 'The Three Faces of Utopianism Revisited'. *Utopian Studies* 5, no. 1 (1994): 1–37.

Sharpe, Christina. *In the Wake: On Blackness and Being*. Duke University Press, 2016.

Sterling, Bruce. 'CATSCAN: Slipstream'. *SF Eye* 5 (1989): 77–80.

Stryker, Susan. 'My Words to Victor Frankenstein above the Village of Chamounix: Performing Transgender Rage'. *GLQ: A Journal of Lesbian and Gay Studies* 1, no. 3 (1994): 237–254.

Suvin, Darko. *Metamorphoses of Science Fiction: On the Poetics and History of a Literary Genre*, ed. Gerry Canavan. Peter Lang, 2016 [1979].

Swanwick, Michael. *The Iron Dragon's Mother*. Tor, 2019.

Wolmark, Jenny. *Aliens and Others: Science Fiction, Feminism and Postmodernism*. University of Iowa Press, 1994.

Further Reading

Academic publications are often very expensive, but many will be available via public and/or university libraries. We have not recommended any studies of individual authors or works, but the *Modern Masters of Science Fiction* (University of Illinois Press) and *SFF: A New Canon* (Palgrave Macmillan) book series are good places to start.

Really useful online resources include www.sf-encyclopedia.com and www.isfdb.org.

Sf histories

Alkon, Paul. *Science Fiction before 1900: Imagination Meets Technology.* Routledge, 2002.

Ashley, Mike. *The Story of the Science-Fiction Magazines.* 5 vols. Liverpool University Press, 2000–2022.

Bould, Mark, and Sherryl Vint. *The Routledge Concise History of Science Fiction.* Routledge, 2011.

Canavan, Gerry, and Eric Carl Link, eds. *The Cambridge History of Science Fiction.* Cambridge University Press, 2019.

James, Edward. *Science Fiction in the Twentieth Century.* Oxford University Press, 1994.

Landon, Brooks. *Science Fiction after 1900: From the Steam Man to the Stars.* Routledge, 2002.

Luckhurst, Roger. *Science Fiction.* Polity, 2005.

Luckhurst, Roger, ed. *Science Fiction: A Literary History.* British Library, 2017.

Roberts, Adam. *The History of Science Fiction.* 2nd ed. Palgrave, 2016.

Stableford, Brian. *New Atlantis: A Narrative History of Scientific Romance.* 4 vols. Wildside Press, 2016.

Stableford, Brian. *The Plurality of Imaginary Worlds: The Evolution of French Roman Scientifique.* Black Coat Press, 2016.

Critical companions, guides and introductions

Bould, Mark. *Science Fiction: The Routledge Film Guidebook.* Routledge 2012.

Bould, Mark, Andrew M. Butler, Adam Roberts and Sherryl Vint, eds. *The Routledge Companion to Science Fiction.* Routledge, 2009.

Bould, Mark, Andrew M. Butler, Adam Roberts and Sherryl Vint, eds. *Fifty Key Figures in Science Fiction.* Routledge, 2009.

James, Edward, and Farah Mendlesohn, eds. *The Cambridge Companion to Science Fiction.* Cambridge University Press, 2003.

Latham, Rob, ed. *Science Fiction Criticism: An Anthology of Essential Writings.* Bloomsbury, 2017.

Latham, Rob, ed. *The Oxford Handbook of Science Fiction.* Oxford University Press, 2014.

Link, Eric Carl, and Gerry Canavan, eds. *The Cambridge Companion to American Science Fiction.* Cambridge University Press, 2015.

Redmond, Sean, ed. *Liquid Metal: The Science Fiction Film Reader.* Wallflower, 2004.

Roberts, Adam. *Science Fiction: The New Critical Idiom.* 2nd ed. Routledge, 2005.

Seed, David, ed. *A Companion to Science Fiction.* Blackwell, 2008.

Telotte, J.P. *Science Fiction Film.* Cambridge University Press, 2001.

Telotte, J.P. *Science Fiction TV.* Routledge 2014.

Telotte, J.P., ed. *The Essential Science Fiction Television Reader.* University Press of Kentucky, 2008.

Vint, Sherryl. *Science Fiction: A Guide for the Perplexed.* Bloomsbury, 2014.

Vint, Sherryl. *Science Fiction: The Essential Knowledge.* MIT Press, 2021.

Vint, Sherryl, ed. *Science Fiction and Cultural Theory: A Reader.* Routledge 2015.

Selected twenty-first-century theory and criticism

Attebery, Brian. *Decoding Gender in Science Fiction.* Routledge, 2002.

Baccolini, Raffaella, and Tom Moylan, eds. *Dark Horizons: Science Fiction and the Dystopian Imagination.* Routledge, 2003.

Banerjee, Anindita. *We Modern People: Science Fiction and the Making of Russian Modernity.* Wesleyan University Press, 2013.

Banerjee, Suparno. *Indian Science Fiction.* University of Wales Press, 2020.

Bellamy, Brent Ryan. *Remainders of the American Century: Post-Apocalyptic Novels in the Age of US Decline.* Wesleyan University Press, 2021.

Bould, Mark, and China Miéville, eds. *Red Planets: Marxism and Science Fiction.* Pluto/Wesleyan University Press, 2009.

Canavan, Gerry, and Kim Stanley Robinson, eds. *Green Planets: Ecology and Science Fiction.* Wesleyan University Press, 2014.

Carrington, André. *Speculative Blackness: The Future of Race in Science Fiction.* University of Minnesota Press, 2016.

Chu, Seo-Young. *Do Metaphors Dream of Literal Sleep? A Science-Fiction Theory of Representation.* Harvard University Press, 2010.

Csicery-Ronay Jr., Istvan. *Mutopia: Science Fiction and Fantastic Knowledge.* Liverpool University Press, 2022.

Csicery-Ronay Jr., Istvan. *The Seven Beauties of Science Fiction.* Wesleyan University Press, 2011.

Freedman, Carl. *Critical Theory and Science Fiction.* Wesleyan University Press, 2000.

Hassler-Forest, Dan. *Science Fiction, Fantasy, and Politics: Transmedia World-Building Beyond Capitalism.* Rowman & Littlefield, 2016.

Haywood Ferreira, Rachel. *The Emergence of Latin American Science Fiction.* Wesleyan University Press, 2011.

Hellekson, Karen. *The Alternate History: Refiguring Historical Time.* Kent State University Press, 2001.

Higgins, David M. *Reverse Colonization: Science Fiction, Imperial Fantasy, and Alt-Victimhood.* University of Iowa Press, 2021.

Hollinger, Veronica, and Joan Gordon, eds. *Edging into the Future: Science Fiction and Contemporary Cultural Transformation.* University of Pennsylvania Press, 2002.

Isaacson, Nathaniel. *Celestial Empire: The Emergence of Chinese Science Fiction.* Wesleyan University Press, 2017.

Khan, Sami Ahmad. *Star Warriors of the Modern Raj: Materiality, Mythology and Technology of Indian Science Fiction.* University of Wales Press, 2021.

Kilgore, DeWitt Douglas. *Astrofuturism: Science, Race, and Visions of Utopia in Space.* University of Pennsylvania Press, 2003.

Langer, Jessica. *Postcolonialism and Science Fiction*. Palgrave Macmillan, 2011.

Lavender III, Isiah. *Afrofuturism Rising: The Literary Prehistory of a Movement*. Ohio State University Press, 2019.

Lavender III, Isiah, and Lisa Yaszek, eds. *Literary Afrofuturism in the Twenty-First Century*. Ohio State University Press, 2020.

Li, Hua. *Chinese Science Fiction during the Post-Mao Cultural Thaw*. University of Toronto Press, 2021.

Mazierska, Ewa, and Alfredo Suppia, eds. *Red Alert: Marxist Approaches to Science Fiction Cinema*. Wayne State University Press, 2016.

Moylan, Tom. *Scraps of the Untainted Sky: Science Fiction, Utopia, Dystopia*. Westview, 2000.

Mukherjee, Upamanyu Pablo. *Final Frontiers: Science Fiction and Techno-Science in Non-Aligned India*. Liverpool University Press, 2020.

Nama, Adilifu. *Black Space: Imagining Race in Science Fiction Film*. University of Texas Press, 2008.

Rieder, John. *Colonialism and the Emergence of Science Fiction*. Wesleyan University Press, 2008.

Rieder, John. *Science Fiction and the Mass Cultural Genre System*. Wesleyan University Press, 2017.

Sanchez-Taylor, Joy. *Diverse Futures: Science Fiction and Authors of Color*. Ohio State University Press, 2021.

Shaviro, Steven. *Discognition*. Repeater, 2016.

Shaviro, Steven. *Extreme Fabulation*. Goldsmiths Press, 2021.

Telotte, J.P. *Animating the Science Fiction Imagination*. Oxford University Press, 2018.

Telotte, J.P. *Movies, Modernism, and the Science Fiction Pulps*. Oxford University Press, 2019.

Vint, Sherryl. *Animal Alterity: Science Fiction and the Question of the Animal*. Liverpool University Press, 2010.

Wittenberg, David. *Time Travel: The Popular Philosophy of Narrative*. Fordham University Press, 2013.

Wittington, William. *Sound Design and Science Fiction*. University of Texas Press, 2007.

Womack, Yatasha. *Afrofuturism: The World of Black Sci-Fi and Fantasy Culture*. Lawrence Hill, 2013.

Yaszek, Lisa. *Galactic Suburbia: Recovering Women's Science Fiction*. Ohio State University Press, 2008.

Yoshinaga, Ida, Sean Guynes and Gerry Canavan, eds. *Uneven Futures: Strategies for Community Survival from Speculative Fiction*. MIT Press, 2022.

About the Contributors

Mark Bould is professor of film and literature at the University of the West of England. His most recent book is *The Anthropocene Unconscious: Climate Catastrophe Culture* (2021).

Rebecca McWilliams Ojala Ballard is assistant professor of English at Florida State University. Her essays have recently appeared in *American Literature*, *ASAP/Journal* and *Science Fiction Studies*.

Gerry Canavan is an associate professor in the English department at Marquette University and author of *Octavia E. Butler* (2016).

David Hartley holds a PhD in creative writing from the University of Manchester and is currently a co-host on the *Autism through Cinema Podcast*.

David M. Higgins is a senior editor for the *Los Angeles Review of Books*, chair of the English Department at Inver Hills College and author of *Reverse Colonization: Science Fiction, Imperial Fantasy, and Alt-Victimhood* (2021).

Sarah Lohmann is a research and teaching fellow at the University of Tübingen in Germany. She is currently preparing her PhD thesis, *The Edge of Time: The Critical Dynamics of Structural Chronotopes in the Utopian Novel*, for publication.

Roger Luckhurst is professor of nineteenth-century studies at Birkbeck College, University of London, and author of *Gothic: An Illustrated History* (2021).

Anna McFarlane is a lecturer in medical humanities at the University of Leeds and author of *Cyberpunk Culture and Psychology: Seeing through the Mirrorshades* (2021).

Aisha Matthews is the managing editor of the *MOSF Journal of Science Fiction*. Her most recent publication is 'Give Me Liberty or Give Me (Double) Consciousness: Literacy, Orality, Print, and the Cultural Formation of Black American Identity in Harriet Jacobs' *Incidents in the Life of a Slave Girl* and Octavia Butler's *Kindred*' in *Third Stone* (2021).

Glyn Morgan is a curator at the Science Museum, London, and his most recent book is *Science Fiction: Voyage to the Edge of Imagination* (2022).

Hugh C. O'Connell is associate professor of English at the University of Massachusetts Boston and editor of *Disputing the Deluge: Collected 21st-Century Writings on Utopia, Narration, and Survival* (2021) by Darko Suvin.

Chris Pak is a lecturer in contemporary writing and digital media at Swansea University and recipient of the British Science Festival's Jacob Bronowski Prize for Science and the Arts (2020).

Col Roche is a 2022 graduate of Southwestern University, where they studied English and Education and completed a research project on queer temporalities in postmodern drama and film.

Joy Sanchez-Taylor is a professor of English at LaGuardia Community College (CUNY) and author of *Diverse Futures: Science Fiction and Authors of Color* (2021).

Steven Shaviro is DeRoy Professor of English at Wayne State University. His most recent books are *Extreme Fabulations: Science Fictions of Life* (2021) and *The Rhythm Image: Music Videos and New Audiovisual Forms* (2022).

Katie Stone researches queer science fiction alongside the Beyond Gender collective. Her most recent article, 'Hungry for Utopia: An Antiwork Reading of Bram Stoker's *Dracula*', can be found in *Utopian Studies*.

Taryne Jade Taylor is an advanced assistant professor of science fiction at Florida Atlantic University, and co-editor of *The Routledge Handbook to CoFuturisms* (forthcoming).

Sherryl Vint is professor of media and cultural studies at the University of California, Riverside. Her most recent book is *Biopolitical Futures in Twenty-First Century Speculative Fiction* (2021).

Elena Welsh graduated in 2022 with a BA in English and feminist studies from Southwestern University, where they completed an honors thesis on YA fantasy literature.

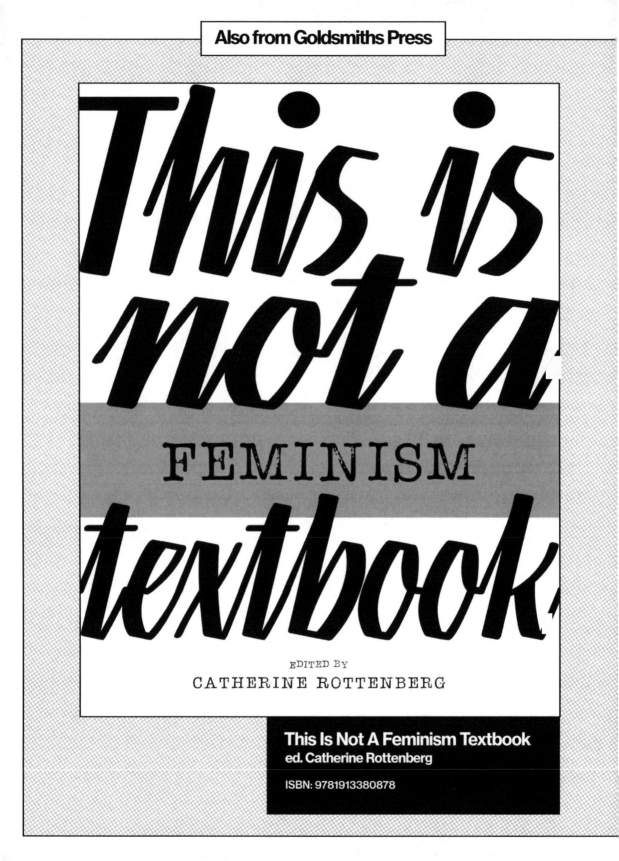

EDITED BY
CATHERINE ROTTENBERG

This Is Not A Feminism Textbook
ed. Catherine Rottenberg

ISBN: 9781913380878

Are smart homes really smart?

Will technology save the world?

What does class have to do with feminism?

And what does 'intersectionality' *actually* mean?

A thought-provoking book written by prominent feminist scholars from around the world. It is engaging and accessible, distilling the highest level of knowledge into fascinating but concise entries.

This Is Not A Feminism Textbook offers a clear, straightforward overview of key feminist debates and concerns ranging from motherhood, home, work and family to media, technology, and medicine.

This book is a must-read for everyone who is curious about the sex/gender distinction, and the relation between gender and other aspects of identity; and it tackles plenty more questions along the way.

With contributions from

Celia Roberts, Amber Jamilla Musser, Simidele Dosekun, Sara R. Farris, Chiara Pellegrini, Cynthia Barounis, Suzanne Leonard, Yolande Strengers, Heather Berg

9781913380618

Empathy

Hoa Pham

GOLD SF°

9781913380786

The Ghostwriters

M.J. Maloney

GOLD SF²

GOLD SF°

Gold SF is a new imprint of Goldsmiths Press, dedicated to discovering and publishing new intersectional feminist science fiction. Science fiction looks to the future and tries to imagine new ways of being in the world. Goldsmiths Press is a natural home for speculative fiction, and this new imprint promotes voices answering to the unprecedented times in which we find ourselves now living.

Series editors: Una McCormack and Paul March-Russell

9781915983053

Merchant

Alexandra Grunberg

GOLD SF°

The Other Shore

Hoa Pham

GOLD SF

Mathematics for Ladies

Poems on Women in Science

Jessy Randall

Foreword by Pippa Goldschmidt
Illustrated by Kristin DiVona

GOLD SF

Little Sisters and Other Stories

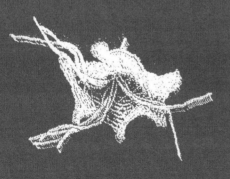

Vonda N. McIntyre

GOLD SF

The Disinformation War

S. J. Groenewegen

GOLD SF